I0552284

Blood of My Blood

"Wrath of The Lion"

ROGER BROWN BOOKS

1st Edition

T.L. BROWNING, AUTHOR, ILLUSTRATOR

WACO, TEXAS

Roger Brown Books
Cover Design/Illustrator: T. L. Browning
Author Photo: T. L. Brown

Library of Congress Control Number: 2020920084

ISBN-13: 978-1-7339061-3-5
Printed in the United States

www.browningtl.com
Facebook.com /browningtl
Instagram/ t.l.browning
Twitter/browningTL3
Twitter/books_roger

Dedications

To my beautiful children,

Jaiden, Jaida & Jonathan

Thank you for being the source of my inspiration and believing in me. I love you with all of my heart. I created this for you so that you will always have your own epic tale with guided words of wisdom.

To my family and friends who have motivated me and encouraged me throughout this journey.

Thank you, thank you, Thank you

Thank you all so much for your love and support.

I love you all.

Table of Contents

"Quiet your mind and calm your

heart, for there is much to be

learned here…"

The little old lady.

Introduction

Blood of My Blood, the sequel to the Jai'Diah series written by T. L. Browning, is a passionate, heart-pounding conclusion to the epic tale of love, pain, and forgiveness. Chapter by chapter Browning grips your heart and does not let go, leaving you gasping for air. This story will stir all of your emotions. Beware, and prepare yourself for a whirlwind of a journey.

T.L. Browning

Chapter 1
The Mantel

Suncomba took his stance, then twirled his spear behind his back as he dug his heels into the dirt. He shouted, "Yah!" as he practiced different fighting moves.

Tungo watched Suncomba from a distance while sitting on a large stone near the waterfall with his legs crossed beneath his robe. He shook his head then stood to his feet, holding a yam in his hand.

"What are you doing?" he yelled.

"Training," Suncomba replied with a puzzled look upon his face.

"No, you are angry!"

"Yes, that too!"

"Battles are not won in anger, so what makes you think you can win a war?"

"They must pay for everything they have done to us, everything they have done to Queen Jai'Diah."

"Yes, they must pay, and they will, but we must use wisdom and understanding to defeat them, not anger."

"Your strength has increased my son. You train well. However, anger will cause you to lose focus and make dangerous mistakes. In war, we cannot afford mistakes. Ask yourself why you must fight."

"I know why I must fight; they destroyed Queen Jai'Diah's family, my family!" Suncomba shouted, breathing heavily.

"Who destroyed them?" Tungo asked.

"I do not know!"

"Why did they destroy them?"

"I do not know!" Suncomba yelled as he threw the spear with such force that it pierced the side of a large tree.

"How can you defeat an enemy you know nothing about?"

Suncomba stared intensely into Tungo's eyes. His heart was pounding, and his breathing rapid. Queen Jai'Diah, who had been sitting in the cave meditating, walked outside to see what was wrong.

"What is going on?" she asked as she stared at Suncomba.

"Everything is ok, my Queen," Suncomba replied as he tried to calm down.

Queen Jai'Diah looked at Tungo.

"Tell me what is going on," she said.

"My Queen, I understand Suncomba's anger towards the enemy, but anger does not win wars, wisdom does. We must understand our enemies to defeat them. Understanding the attack on your family will help us plan a strategy to defeat them."

"What do you know about your enemies, my Queen?"

"I know that the leader wears a long black hooded robe. He rode on the back of a monstrous beast, and his magical hands shot flames of fire. One thing that has bothered me since the attack is that the leader continued to pursue me after he destroyed our kingdom. His creature took the Golden Book of Knowledge from me. It would have killed me had you not saved my life. Did they kill my family because of me, because of the Golden Book?"

"My Queen, I am afraid so, and you are not out of danger yet. The Golden Book of Knowledge is the most powerful book known to man. You are the Guardian of the Golden Book of Knowledge; therefore, its great power can only be revealed through you. By now, the enemy knows this and has his creatures combing through the lands looking for you. They are coming for you, my Queen."

Jai'Diah took a deep breath then exhaled.

"Why is this book so important?" Suncomba asked. Tungo sat back down on the stone and removed a dagger from inside his waistband. He began to peel his yam.

"Come, have a seat," he said

Queen Jai'Diah and Suncomba sat down on the ground in front of the large stone. They listened carefully to Tungo as he began to speak.

"Many years ago, Yahweh spoke through his Chosen Few, who wrote powerful messages in the Golden Book of Knowledge at his request. This book was the spoken Word of God. It held his thoughts and commandments. In this book, Yahweh spoke of his unconditional love for us, his chosen people. He expressed his will over our lives. Many unbelievers came against the Chosen Few of Yahweh. They wanted the chosen to stop teaching from the book. Some of the unbelievers became so angry, they vowed to destroy the book and kill those who taught from it, but this was not the Will of Yahweh. To protect this precious book, he covered it with his seal of protection, his Spirit, and cloaked it in Gold; this is how it became known as the Golden Book of Knowledge. The Indestructible Powerful Word of Yahweh. For an exceedingly long time, a few lifetimes in, fact, unbelievers sought to destroy the book because it taught against their devilishly wicked ways. Those who taught others what they had learned from the Golden Book of Knowledge were often imprisoned or killed. Teachers of the Golden Book had to flee their homes to save themselves from the wrath of the unbelievers. One evening one of the Chosen Few, a young man, was awakened from his nap by a soft whisper. The voice told him to arise and journey north. There was something special about the voice. It warmed the Chosen in such a way that he knew without a doubt that it was the Almighty One. The man packed a few items, then headed out on his journey north. He traveled many days and nights, not knowing exactly where he was going or what he would have to do when he got there. All he knew was that Yahweh said go, and he had to go. At one point along the journey, the man got tired and weary. He began to second guess what Yahweh had spoken to him. He began to wonder if he had made it all up in his head. The man called out to the Almighty One for an answer. Tears streamed down his cheeks as he stared up into the heavens. He then fell to his knees and laid face down against the earth. He said, "Yahweh, I need to know that you are with me. Please answer me. I have journeyed for so long, and I am tired and confused. Show me the way. Guide me, father," the man said as he cried out to Yahweh.

"Look up, my son," a quiet voice replied. "You are here."

The man lifted his head, and in the distance, he saw a soft glow of light. The man got up from the ground and wiped his face. He picked up his satchel and started running towards the glowing light. He panted, and his heart was racing. He was not afraid. He was excited. Drawing closer, he slowed down to the point of walking. As he approached the light, he noticed that it was coming from inside what appeared to be a small entrance into a tunnel. The man did not hesitate. He immediately knelt down and crawled inside the tunnel. It was a tight fit at first; however, the further the man descended into the tunnel, the wider it became, ultimately leading to a vast underground cave. Suddenly a voice spoke.

"Here, I will teach you. Here you will train others in my ways. I will lead them here. Where you are with me, the world knoweth not. Be not afraid; I will help thee."

"Yes, Father," the servant replied as he bowed his head.

"As the voice became silent, the man surveyed the cave. He noticed two large fruit trees growing in the middle of the cave. Between the trees, a river of crystal-clear water flowed. As he stared into the water, something caught his eye. Something glistened beneath the surface. It was the Golden Book of Knowledge. The man slowly reached his hand into the water and retrieved the book. As he held it in his hands, his eyes widened in astonishment. He then sat down on a large stone near the edge of the river. He opened the book and began to read aloud. As the man studied the book, he became more knowledgeable in the ways of Yahweh. Over time, Yahweh led individuals from different tribes to the sacred cave, where they grew in wisdom, knowledge, and understanding. These chosen few pledged their devotion and loyalty to Yahweh. They studied relentlessly, the Golden Book of Knowledge and developed a deep relationship with the Almighty One. This group of individuals which represented the twelve tribes of Africa became known as the Mantel, and the place where they trained was known as the Veil in Hadriel. After being taught the ways of Yahweh, each one returned to his and her tribes. They taught their tribes the ways of the Almighty. No one dared to challenge or persecute them for even those who were unbelievers knew that there was something special about those who were a part of the Mantel. The Mantel was respected throughout the country. Kings and Queens, near and far, sought their guidance," Tungo continued.

"You see my Queen; this Golden Book is precious. It is the most valuable gift on earth, and you were chosen to use it. You must lead the people back to the Almighty One, God, our Father. Because so many have sought to destroy it or use it for evil, Yahweh covered it with his Spirit. Because of this, it is written in a language known only by you, its Guardian, and Yahweh."

"How do you know that I know this language in which you speak of?" Queen Jai'Diah asked. "I have told no one."

"I know because Yahweh has shown me," Tungo replied. "He revealed this to me so that I would be able to help you understand your purpose and why your enemy is pursuing you. Your time is now! You must stand strong and fight, for this enemy is great. He has the Golden Book of Knowledge. However, he knows that it is of no use to him without you to translate it."

"But if it is the Word of Yahweh and meant to be used for the good of his people, how can it be of use to my enemy?" Queen Jai'Diah asked.

"My Queen, your enemy is clever and desire to rule over all the earth. To do so, he must manipulate the Word of Yahweh. He plans to use it to trick the people into believing what he says is true, yet it will not be the truth. He will twist it for his evil motives. Good will become evil, and evil will become good. If he captures you, he will do everything in his power to force you to denounce the truth written in the Golden Book of Knowledge. He will change the wording to something more to his liking. First, he must know what is written in the book. That is why I must protect you. That is why we must be prepared. War is coming, and we must be ready," answered Tungo.

"We cannot defeat this enemy alone for we are few, and he has many," Suncomba said.

"We are not alone; we have Yahweh," Tungo replied. "We have brothers and sisters near and far who are with us. We have The Mantel."

"You speak of The Mantel, yet you also spoke as though they were few in numbers," Suncomba replied.

"Yes, I spoke of the origin which was many years ago. The body of believers has grown; therefore, so has The Mantel. My brother, if the numbers were few, would not Yahweh be yet enough? Do not let doubt enter your heart. Strengthen your faith, for Yahweh is mighty alone."

"My faith is strong; however, no one yet speaks of The Mantel," Suncomba replied. "Why have they been silent for so long? What happened?"

Chapter 2
Fire & Ice

Tungo stares into Suncomba's eyes, then turns his head towards the beautiful waterfall. He was reluctant to speak on it, but he did.

"What happened to The Mantel is a past that I rather not remember," Tungo said, "nevertheless, I must, for it is something that you must know to understand the importance of what we are preparing for at this very moment. It is painful for me to relive, yet relive it, I must."

Tungo turned his head back towards Suncomba and Queen Jai'Diah. He looked them in the eyes, then began to tell what happened.

"After Yahweh spoke to his servant, one of the chosen few, The Mantel began to take form. Those who were chosen came from near and far to study the ways of Yahweh under The Veil. The Mantel used the knowledge and gifts given to them by the Almighty to help their tribes grow and prosper. For many years, the twelve tribes prospered under the rule of The Mantel. Of the twelve tribes, the tribes of Fire and Ice were the largest and strongest tribes. The tribes of Fire and Ice were the twelve tribes of Africa's primary defense against any outside forces. When they fought alone, they were great; however, when their forces combined, they were unstoppable. Every outside force that rose against the armies of Fire and Ice were destroyed. Their power was undeniable. Though there were twelve tribes, these two tribes upheld Africa, for they were the source of its strength. Everyone was glad to have the tribes of Fire and Ice as their protection, everyone but Abe that is."

"Who was Abe?" asked Queen Jai'Diah

"Abe was one of The Mantel's Elect. He was short in stature, dark-skinned with bushy brown hair. He had a long, braided bead, and three long tribal scars on his cheek. He was a strong-willed, vigilant man who craved power. Abe held himself high above the other Elect. Although he, was from the tribe of Ice, Abe believed that the tribes of Fire and Ice held too much power, all of which he wanted for himself. He was extremely jealous of Mazena and Kaijo, leaders of the Fire and

Ice Tribes. Mazena was the Officer of War for the Tribe of Ice. She was a gorgeous woman with beauty and strength. Mazena's hair was thick, which she kept half braided down one side with tribal beads at the end. The other half of her head was shaved with distinctive patterns painted on her scalp. Her skin was unique and quite lovely to look upon. It was as if night and day were interwoven. Splashes of light adorn her gorgeous brown skin. Her eyes were as rare as her skin. Graced with unique beauty, she had one blue eye and one the color of golden honey which looked as though a starburst of fire danced inside. Everyone was captivated by Mazena's beauty, for she was truly a rare gem, and so was her heart. Her strength was mighty, though she had a humble spirit. The warmth of Mazena's soul magnified her outer beauty, and that is what captured Kaijo's heart. Kaijo, the leader of the Fire Tribe, was also an Officer of War. He was a brilliant warrior who specialized in battle strategy. He was tall, broad, brown-skinned, with striking muscular features. His eyes were grey and fierce as if a storm were brewing inside of them. Some would say he had the strength of one hundred men. However, none of his strength mattered when he was around Mazena, for he became utterly weak at the sight of her. She held his heart prisoner and did not know it. The two fought and planned battle strategies together. They eventually started spending time together off the battlefield. Mazena soon fell in love with Kaijo, and he fell for her as well. They spent much time sharing walks and talking about life. They had more in common than war. They both enjoyed watching the sunset and sitting under the night sky, discussing the wonders of the stars. Sometimes they met up secretly to have dinner together. Mazena and Kaijo spent so much time together that someone inside The Mantel had growing concerns that Mazena and Kaijo were becoming far too close and shunning everyone else in The Mantel. That someone was Abe. He did not like what he saw, for it was something that he could not control. Abe loved being in control. He enjoyed feeling important and powerful. He feared that Mazena and Kaijo's growing friendship would interfere with his plans, plans to one day become the leader of The Mantel. He desired to one day rule over all twelve tribes. Abe had long thought of his plan. The rest of the Mantel's Elect thought of Abe as stern, but a man of sound judgment, therefore; they respected him. They looked to Abe for counsel before finalizing any decisions regarding issues or concerns within the twelve tribes. Because of this, Abe deemed himself as the highest ranking of all the Elect within The Mantel. Even though every Elect was considered equal, Abe did not see it that way. He knew that Mazena and Kaijo had the potential to be a major flaw in his plan. In an attempt to prevent Mazena and Kaijo from growing closer, Abe approached The Mantel with his growing concern of the friendship between the two. He explained to the Elect that because the Tribes of Fire and Ice were so great, it would be dangerous for Mazena and Kaijo to grow any closer. If they ever decided to do so, the two could one day join forces and rule merciless over the remaining ten tribes. Abe told the Elect that bad things would surely follow if the friendship between Mazena and Kaijo were not broken immediately. Abe said that The Mantel must intervene. Although the Elect of The Mantel valued Abe's wisdom and knowledge, they did not agree with him on this matter. They knew Mazena and Kaijo were well-respected leaders, warriors who had always defended The Mantel and the twelve tribes of Africa. The Elect had no reason not to trust Mazena and Kaijo. The leaders had proven themselves to be trustworthy; therefore, The Mantel dismissed Abe's request that the friendship between the leaders of the Fire and Ice Tribe be broken. As the rest of the Elect dismissed themselves from the meeting, Abe stood there, all alone in disbelief. This angered him deeply. The Mantel had always heeded his advice; however, they turned their backs on him. It infuriated Abe. He aimed to rule the twelve tribes, but the bond between Mazena and Kaijo threatened his plans. Abe could not let them wreck his plan to rule. He began to think of a way to break the bond between Mazena and Kaijo. Abe began to follow Mazena and Kaijo; however, he found nothing he could use against them; this angered him more. Because he found no wrongdoing, Abe made up a lie then asked The Mantel to meet with him once more. Once the Elect gathered under The Veil, Abe told them that he had been following Mazena and Kaijo for some time. Abe informed The Mantel that Mazena and Kaijo were joining together. He told the Elect that he overheard Kaijo tell Mazena that the Tribes of Fire and Ice would become all-powerful and have dominion over all of Africa. Abe told The Mantel that Kaijo and Mezena would soon demand all of the tribes to serve them. The more Abe spoke of Mazena and Kaijo's alleged plan, the more the Elect became uneasy. Slowly, more of the Elect became fearful of the possibilities. Some of them began to watch Mazena and Kaijo in secret. Those who watched reported back to The Mantel what they had found. Mazena and Kaijo had no idea they were being watched, so they went on with their life, for they had nothing to hide and nothing to fear. The two spent countless hours talking and enjoying one another's company. They even trained together. One evening while training with their spears, Mazena told Kaijo not to go easy on her because she was a woman, but to fight her like the true warrior she was. Kaijo agreed, and he would not let up as he fought Mazena. Mazena held her ground until a powerful strike across her back from Kaijo's spear landed her on the ground. Breathing heavily, Mazena stumbled as she tried to get up. Out of deep concern, Kaijo hurried over to assist Mazena. However, Mazena had other plans as she quickly leaped to her feet. She twirled her spear behind her back then swung it across the back of Kaijo's legs, knocking them from under him. Kaijo hit the ground so hard it seemed as though the earth shook beneath him. Mazena then stood over him with one foot on his chest and her spear pointed downward at him. Their eyes locked in such an intense gaze. Words cannot describe what their hearts felt at that moment. Mazena reached out her hand to help Kaijo up. Kaijo grabbed ahold of Mazena's hand and jumped to his feet. Once face to face, they could not stop gazing into each other's eyes. Kaijo took his hand and stroked the side of Mazena's cheek and said."

"You are the most beautiful woman I have ever seen."

Mazena smiled and said, "You mean warrior."

Cupping Mazena's chin in his hand, Kaijo said, "Yes, and I am in love with them both. Does the warrior mind if I share a kiss with this beautiful woman?"

Mazena replied, "She does not mind at all."

"The two then shared the most passionate kiss beneath the purple and amber skies," Tungo said. "This was the beginning of something oh so beautiful. Unbeknownst to

Mazena and Kaijo, they were being watched. Two of the Elects witnessed what happened and became fearful. They thought about what Abe had told them in The Veil. The danger seemed a bit more realistic after seeing with their own eyes how close Mazena and Kaijo had grown. The two-Elect hurried back to The Veil and informed the others of what they had witnessed. Fearful, The Mantel began to devise a plan to separate Kaijo and Mazena, which pleased Abe greatly. Meanwhile, Mazena and Kaijo, still unaware of what was going on around them, continued to grow closer. After seeing that Mazena felt the same way about him, Kaijo sat down with her and shared his sincere feelings."

He said, "Mazena, I know that I am looked upon as one of the bravest warriors of the twelve tribes. I know that there is no war that I would not fight, no war that I could not win, for I have been gifted incredible strength and skills. Yet, when I am near you, none of this matter for in your presence, my strength fails me. I become weak. I have never felt this way before. It is difficult for me to explain. I do not understand it. I only know that although your presence weakens me, I find my strength in knowing that for you, I would fight an endless war. The love I have for you…"

"Love," Mazena interrupted. "You love me?" she asked as she stared into Kaijo's eyes.

"Yes, I love you," Kaijo answered as he took Mazena's hands in his.

Tears streamed down Mazena's face as she continued to gaze into Kaijo's eyes.

"What is wrong?" Kaijo asked.

"Nothing is wrong." Mazena replied, "Nothing is wrong at all."

Kaijo wiped the tears from Mazena's eyes. As he did so, Mazena took his hands as she looked into his eyes.

"I love you too." She said.

Kaijo smiled at her as he kissed Mazena's hand.

"Marry me?" He asked.

Mazena smiled and agreed to marry Kaijo.

"The following evening, as the sun began to set, Kaijo and Mazena, each alone in their separate huts dressed in gorgeous ceremonial robes. Mazena wore a lovely red robe with gold and black embroidered designs. A strand of golden beads hung from her waist, and golden bangles danced around her ankles. She looked radiant. With her hair roped into a braid of red and gold threads, Mazena was a sight to behold. After she dressed, she knelt on her mat and began to pray. She was happy, and thanked Yahweh for the joy he had brought to her life, Kaijo. Not too far away in another hut, Kaijo knelt in prayer, giving glory to Yahweh for Mazena, the calm to his storm, for she was the peace in his rage. Dressed in a black and gold robe, with his face and arms decorated in tribal paint, Kaijo prepared for the upcoming ceremony. The sun had almost set; it was now time for Kaijo and Mazena to be on their way. As the sunset turned the sky amber and gold, Kaijo and Mazena made their way to the home of the Great Priest. Mazena and Kaijo were happy in love and excited about their blessed union as man, wife, and warriors. After hearing the news of Mazena and Kaijo's secret marriage ceremony, The Mantel became more disturbed than before. They feared the power that Kaijo and Mazena held. For if Mazena and Kaijo's tribes ever rebelled against The Mantel, they would be unstoppable. Abe and the other Elect officers of The Mantel kept their grave concerns at bay for quite some time. After a while, many of the Elects' concerns slowly disappeared as they continued to secretly watch Mazena and Kaijo. The Elect saw that Kaijo and Mazena were truly in love and knew that their intentions were pure; it was made all the clearer when Mazena gave birth to a beautiful baby, a son named Jabari. All loved him, for he was such a sweet child. Mazena and Kaijo loved Jabari with all of their hearts and vowed to always protect him. Watching from a distance, Abe saw the happiness and love in Mazena and Kaijo's eyes. He meant to pluck it out by any means necessary. He could not rely on the help of the rest of the Elect because they all had become quite fond of Mazena and Kaijo. Abe tried to explain to The Mantel that Mazena and Kaijo's tribes were more of the risk now than ever before because they were joined permanently by the blood of their son, Jabari. After hearing this, some of the Elect demanded that a vote be cast to end the absurd allegations and secret watch of Mazena and Kaijo. The Mantel agreed that once the vote was cast, if no one agreed with Abe, then his quest to destroy Mazena and Kaijo's relationship must come to an end. If the Mantel favored Abe, then a compromise would be made. Mazena and Kaijo's tribe would be forced to agree to the terms of The Mantel. All of this happened without Mazena and Kaijo's knowledge. The couple was still enjoying the bliss of their union. With no war on the horizon, everything was wonderful between the twelve tribes. There was peace throughout the land. Back at The Veil, the vote was cast. The Elect from every tribe voted against Abe. Abe, who was a member of Kaijo's tribe, was furious. The anger within him burned with the intensity of the sun. Abe could not believe that not one person sided with him. How could they not see the danger, he asked himself. He stood up quickly and addressed The Mantel."

"You will soon regret this decision!" he shouted and stormed off.

"Abe went back home to his tribe; there, he sat in his compound and thought of a wicked plan. He decided to kill Mazena and Kaijo himself. The more Abe thought about it, the darker his heart became. He set his plan into motion. He waited quite some time, years in fact, before executing it to prevent The Mantel from being suspicious of him. Kaijo and Mazena enjoyed their family, unaware that they were in great danger. The tribes were at peace, and there were no outside threats. Kaijo and Mazena had no reason to be wary of danger, or so they thought. They did not know of the threat within their midst. They had always viewed The Veil as a group of wise leaders who followed the teachings of Yahweh. However, there was one who had fallen, one who had given into the unquenchable thirst of power. A jackal was in their midst. Abe knew that Kaijo and Mazena were great warriors. Hand to hand combat was not an option, for he would not last one second against either of them. Instead of hand to hand combat, Abe decided to poison them. He knew it would work, for everyone was at peace with each other. There was no reason to fear or distrust anyone. One night before super Abe went to visit Mazena and Kaijo. Once he arrived at the compound, he bowed before them. The couple invited him inside. Upon entering Mazena and Kaijo's home, Abe told them that he wanted to share with them some ideas he had that would help strengthen their tribes all the more. Knowing that Abe was a wise man of The Mantel, it was extremely easy for Mazena and Kaijo to trust him. Abe gave the couple a jug of palm wine as a gift for receiving him into their home. It was customary that if someone were given the gifts or food or drink, it would be shared amongst them as to show thanks for the gift. Abe sat down with Mazena and Kaijo. They drank palm wine together; however, Abe only pretended to drink the wine. As Abe spoke of his ideas for the tribe, Mazena became ill. She felt dizzy and fainted. Kaijo rushed over to her side, trying hard to wake her up. Abe tried to wake her as well; however, he knew it was of no use. Kaijo told Abe to stay with his wife while he went to get help. Abe insisted that Kaijo stay with Mazena, telling him that he would get help instead. Kaijo agreed. He knelt back down near his wife and continued trying to wake her. Soon after, Kaijo began to feel ill as well. As he tried to speak, he fell over across his wife's chest and did not wake up. Abe stared down at them both with an evil smile upon his face then took the jug of palm wine to cover his tracks, after which he left the compound never to return there again. Later the next day, one of Mazena's warriors went by to see if everything was ok because Mazena did not show up to train her warriors that morning. That was highly unusual. As she approached the compound, she heard a child crying. The warrior immediately knew it was the voice of Jabari. She knew something was wrong, so she raced to the compound, leaping over the gate. She hurried inside only to find Mazena and Kaijo dead. Their son, Jabari, was kneeling on the floor crying for his parents. The warrior stood in shock as she stared at the scene before her. Jabari turned and looked up at the warrior. His eyes were swollen, and his face stained with tears from crying so much. Jabari quickly stood up and ran to the warrior."

Hugging her tightly around the waist, he looked up and said, "I cannot wake them."

The warrior held Jabari close as tears flowed from her eyes. She quickly wiped the tears away then knelt in front of Jabari.

"Listen to me." She said. "I know that you are sad, but we have to go. We have to leave this place. I have to take you somewhere safe. It is not safe for you to stay here."

"I do not want to go; I want to stay with them!" Jabari shouted.

"My child, you cannot stay here. It is dangerous. We do not know who did this, and they may come back for you." The warrior replied.

Jabari became quiet, for he was afraid. He looked at the warrior as he wiped the tears from his eyes.

"Where will we go?" Jabari asked as he continued to sniff, trying to keep from crying again.

"I know someone who will protect and guard you with their life. Hurry, gather your most treasured things; we must leave this place at once. Jabari gathered a few things from his hut, and as he was leaving, he walked over to where his mother and father lay. He took his father's gold and brass cuffs from his arms. Jabari then turned to his mother and removed the necklace from her neck and the dagger from her waistband. A tear fell from his eye and streamed down his cheek as he turned and walked out of the compound. The warrior was waiting for him by the gate with two spears and a sword in her hand. It was his mother and father's weapons."

"Your parents would have wanted you to have these," the warrior said. "You will need them someday; of that, I am certain."

Jabari tried to take his father's sword into his hand, but it was far too heavy.

"One day, I will be a great warrior like my father and mother. I will make the person who did this pay," Jabari said sternly.

"Yes, you will," the warrior agreed.

They both then left the compound and never returned.

Chapter 3
Blood of My Blood

J abari watched from a distance as dark black smoke rose to the sky near his family compound. Drums and chanting could be heard as warriors from the Tribes of Fire and Ice celebrated the lives of both Mazena and Kaijo in a traditional burial ceremony. Jabari could not bring himself to attend, for he said within his heart the day he left the compound, that he would never return. Though he had many great memories of his time with his mother and father, the memory of his loss was the one his heart could not bear, therefore, he refused to relive it. As Jabari continued looking up at the smoke, he felt rage growing dark like the cloud of smoke rising in the sky.

Rage from a broken heart cannot be contained. It spreads wild like fire on the driest of plains. Jabari lifted his hands to the sky and let out a great cry, then fell to the ground in tears. Soon he felt a steady, firm grip on his shoulder.

"It is ok, my son," a voice said. "Let it all out. If you do not, it will eat you alive. You must learn how to channel the anger that is within you. You must control it."

"I do not want to control it!" Jabari shouted. "I want to use it to kill the one who took them from me!"

"That will not bring them back, nor will it bring you any peace. You will still be lost, my son."

"I don't care! I will have my revenge!"

"Yes, my son, vengeance will come but not now, not this way. We do not know who committed this evil act against your family. We must be patient as we continue to search for the enemy."

"I do not want to wait!"

"Are you willing to risk the lives of the innocent to get your revenge? Do you want innocent blood on your hands?"

"No," Jabari replied with his head hung low.

Jabari arose from the ground. He turned around to see who it was that had touched him. An older man with long white locs and a bushy grey beard stood before him. The man had dark brown eyes, and his skin was the color of bronze. His skin glistened in the light of the sun.

He was a brawny man. To Jabari, he looked like a giant. His arms were as thick as the branches of a Baobabs tree. That is what he reminded Jabari of, a Baobabs tree, The Tree of Life.

"Who are you?" Jabari asked.

"I am Kei, the Great Priest," Kei replied. "I knew your mother and your father. I joined them in union before you came unto this world. They were skilled warriors, but more importantly, they possessed kind and loving hearts. My son, you are the perfect combination of both of your parents, Fire and Ice. You possess their noble qualities, but you do not know how to use them correctly, yet. I will teach you."

"I do not need you to teach me!" Jabari yelled.

"You do need him." Someone else answered.

Jabari turned to see who it was that spoke to him. It was the warrior who rescued him from the compound.

"Jabari remember when I told you that I knew someone who would protect you, this is he. Kei is a Great Priest who also trained as a powerful warrior. He is the one who trained your mother. He will take care of you and protect you with his very life."

Surprised at what he had just learned, Jabari walked over to Kei.

"Is this true?"

"Yes, my son, it is true."

T. L. Browning

"Your mother was one of my greatest students."

"Will you train me as you trained her?"

"Yes, in due time. It is not something that happens overnight. It takes time, commitment, and patience. Are you willing to listen and obey me?"

"Yes, I am."

"Are you sure?" asked Kei

"Yes, I am sure." Jabari responded.

"This will not come easy, because of your heartbreak, it will be most difficult indeed."

"Teach me." Jabari pleaded.

Kei gazed deeply into Jabari's eyes, then turned and walked away. Jabari stood there in disappointment.

"Are you just going to stand there, or are you coming with me?" Kei asked as he turned around and looked at Jabari.

Jabari ran to catch up with Kei.

"Come along now. I want you to meet my son, Muji. You both are around the same age. He has just begun his training. You will train with him."

"Not long after, Jabari began to train with Muji. The two trained hard. Out of all the warriors Kei trained, Muji and Jabari were the best. They often competed against each other as they trained to be seen as the best in Kei's eyes. Though their competition was fierce, Jabari and Muji were the best of

~ 30 ~

friends. As time passed, they became as close as brothers; in fact, they saw each other as brothers. They eventually stopped competing against each other. Instead, they fought alongside each other. They always protected and defended one another. Jabari and Muji grew into strong, handsome young men. Meanwhile, inside The Veil, Abe had elevated himself above all the Elect. No one took a stand against him out of guilt. The Elect believed that had they listened to Abe from the beginning, Kaijo and Mazena would have lived. The Elect faulted themselves; therefore, they did not argue with Abe when he suggested himself as the head Elect of The Veil. Unbeknownst to the rest of the Elect, Abe was the one who killed Kaijo and Mazena. Although Kaijo and Mazena were no more, Abe still considered their son Jabari a threat to his position of power. Jabari was the sole blood tie to the Tribes of Fire and Ice. Abe's guilty conscious led him to believe that Jabari would one day be his downfall. He watched in secret as Jabari trained. His concerns deepened as Jabari grew to be the most powerful warrior."

"He is getting far too strong," Abe whispered to himself. "I must destroy him now."

"Once again, Abe set his evil plan into motion. That night, Abe gathered the ingredients needed to create the same poison he used to kill Jabari's parents. Not very far away, as he lay sleeping within his compound, Kei was awakened by the most disturbing dream. The dream warned him of an attempt on Jabari's and Muji's life. The dream frightened Kei, for he loved Muji and Jabari with all of his heart. He would not let any harm come to them. Kei quickly got up and ran to Jabari and Muji's hut. He shook them until they awoke."

"Wake up! Wake up!" Kei whispered sternly. "You must get up!"

Muji and Jabari finally awoke.

"What is the matter, father?" Muji asked

"You both are in danger. You must hurry and leave now." Kei answered

"In danger from who?" Jabari asked.

"I am not sure, but I have an idea."

"Your dream, it was Abe?" Jabari asked.

"Yes, but how did you know?" Kei asked, in dismay.

"I saw him in mine, and it helped me remember more about the night my parents died. I remember Abe coming to visit them that night about some ideas he had for the tribes. I know I was much younger at the time, but I remember it as though it was recent as yesterday."

"My son, you are correct in your thinking," Kei replied.

"I have long suspected Abe, but I was uncertain until this very moment. He sees you as a threat just as he once saw your mother and father. That is why he wants you dead. Your blood joins the mighty tribes of Fire and Ice together; therefore, you hold more power than he ever could. That is why you must hurry and leave this place now."

"No, I will kill him first!" Jabari yelled.

"No, you will not. You must not be tied to this in any way in order to protect your parents' honor and your future as the leader of the tribes. Only a member of the Elect can handle a situation such as this. I am one of the Elects."

"Jabari was not happy with Kei's decision for he wanted his revenge; however, he understood the tribal order of things. He did not want to dishonor his parents' memory; therefore, he reluctantly stepped aside and allowed Kei to stand in his place." After gathering their things, Jabari and Muji walked toward the gate of the compound. They stopped short of the gate and turned towards Kei. Kei walked over to Muji and hugged him. As tears fell from his eyes, he told his son and Jabari that he loved them. Soon after, Kei sent them on their way. Muji and Jabari promised to return, afterwards, they ran off into the night under the shadow of the fluorescent moon. Later, after watching them until he could no longer see their shadows bounce off the light of the moon, Kei went back inside the compound. He wept, for he did not know when or if he would see Muji and Jabari again. Shortly after, Kei wiped away his tears and made ready for a most expected visit from Abe. With his sword in hand, Kei sat on a mat with his legs folded beneath him in the center of his compound. He waited and meditated throughout the rest of the night and on into the next day. That evening as Kei waited patiently; he heard a loud shout from the gate. With his sword at his side, Kei went out to see who called out to him. As he drew closer, he could see Abe standing at the gate with a jug of palm wine in his hands."

He greeted Kei with a friendly smile upon his face, then said, "Kei, my dear brother, I have come to visit with you concerning Jabari. I have brought with me this jug of Palm wine as a gift to praise him for his dedication to becoming a great warrior. I have heard the wonderful news of his progress and wanted to congratulate him myself."

"Jabari is not here." Kei replied with a serious look upon his face.

Abe stood at the gate puzzled.

"What do you mean he is not here?" Abe asked as he looked around the compound as far as his eyes could see.

"Does he not live here? Call for Muji so I can ask him where Jabari has gone."

"Muji is not here," Kei answered as he stared coldly into Abe's eyes.

"Where is he?"

"Gone, far away from here."

"You lie!" Abe shouted. "They are here, let me speak to them!"

"They are not here. I sent Jabari and Muji away from this place."

"Why?" Abe asked.

"To get away from you."

"Me!" Abe replied, appearing shocked by Kei's response.

"Yes, you. We know that it was you who killed Jabari's mother and father."

Abe became angry. His heart pounded as rage boiled in his veins.

"What?" Abe shouted. "I did no such thing. You cannot prove…

"The boy remembers," Kei interrupted.

Abe stopped talking and just stared angrily at Kei.

"He remembers everything," Kei said as he stared back at Abe.

Abe just stood there, panting with his nostrils flaring as though he were a dragon.

"So why did you come here?" Kei asked. "Is it to poison Jabari like you did his mother and father?"

"You cannot prove anything!" Abe shouted

While continuing to stare into Abe's eyes, Kei walked over to Abe. Abe, who had one hand on the dagger hidden inside his robe, was ready to strike Kei if necessary. They both stood there, staring each other down. Suddenly Kei reached out and snatched the jug of Palm wine from Abe's hand.

"This is all the proof I need when I go before The Mantel," Kei replied.

"Abe stood in shock for a moment as Kei turned and walked away. After realizing what had just taken place, Abe ran behind Kei and stabbed him in the back. Kei cried out in pain. As he stumbled forward trying to regain his balance, Kei quickly pulled his sword from its sheath. He then swung around with his sword in his hand, and with all his strength, he severed Abe's head from his body. Kei then fell to the ground. Later that evening, Kei and Abe were found on the ground near the gate. Abe was dead, of course, but Kei yet had life in him. Kei was quickly picked up from the ground to be taken to the tribal healer. Before he was carried away, Kei asked one of his tribal brothers to bring him the jug of Palm wine. The brother brought it to Kei. Although it was almost empty, Kei held onto the jug tightly as he was carried off to the tribal healer. Fortunately, there was enough inside the jug to prove that Abe intended to poison Jabari, as he did Kaijo and Mazena. After learning all that had transpired, the Elect of The

Mantel was torn. Although Abe was an evil and devilish man, many refused to believe he would go to such lengths to destroy prominent leaders such as Mazena and Kaijo. Others sided with Kei, for they knew he was an honorable man who would protect his family from all those who would do them harm, even a fellow Elect of the Mantel. This most horrible offense divided The Mantel beyond reconciliation, thus separating the twelve tribes, causing a great rift between the Tribes of Fire and Ice. Until this day, the Fire and Ice Tribes blame each other for what happened to Mazena and Kaijo."

Chapter 4
Lost, Found, & Lost Again

Tears rolled down Queen Jai'Diah's cheeks as Tungo finished telling the story of what happened to The Mantel. After he finished, Tungo climbed down from the large stone where he was sitting. He stretched, for he had been sitting for quite a while. Suncomba sat in silence as Queen Jai'Diah wiped the tears from her cheeks. Tungo turned and walked towards the waterfall.

"What happened to Kei, Muji, and Jabari?" Suncomba called out as Tungo walked away.

Tungo stopped in his tracks as he looked at the waterfall.

"Kei healed from his wound and continued to serve as an Elect of The Mantel until he passed from this life. Before he passed, his son Muji, and Jabari visited him every chance they could. Because hatred between the tribes had grown immensely, Muji and Jabari only traveled home under the light of the moon. They were like shadows in the night. Upon their visits, Kei continued to use wisdom, knowledge, and understanding to guide and teach them. Muji and Jabari visited, until Kei, in his old age, on his dying bed, forbade them from ever returning out of fear for their safety. Jabari and Muji promised Kei they would honor his wishes. After Kei passed to the next life, Muji and Jabari watched the ceremony from a distance just as Jabari had watched his parent's ceremony when he was a child. After the ceremony, Muji and Jabari vowed to remain brothers and be there for each other always. The two then went their separate ways, for they had much to learn on their own. Muji never married but continued training in the art of warfare. He taught others as well. He formed a secret warrior brotherhood to protect the twelve tribes from any outside forces or internal threats. Muji's heart was pure, and he desired to protect Yahweh's people. It is said that he was visited by an unknown warrior from above, one unlike any this world has ever seen. This warrior taught Muji skills and techniques unknown to any man. It is believed, the warrior gifted Muji with special abilities because his heart was pure. The unknown warrior appeared, and Muji disappeared. No one knows where he went or if he is still alive. After Jabari and Muji said their goodbyes, Jabari traveled afar until he found a small village. There he met a beautiful young woman name Nema. Nema was tall with beautiful dark skin that glistened like stars against a black night sky. She had such a lovely smile and eyes the color of bronze. Her hair was short, black, and full of tight curls. She was sure a beauty, Jabari, fell for Nema immediately. She fell for him as well. Not long after, the two were married. Months later, Nema gave birth to a baby boy. The boy was loved and cherished by his mother and father. As the little boy grew, Jabari began to train him at an early age. Jabari knew the importance of his bloodline and that some still sought to do him harm; therefore, he trained his son and his wife as warriors. He taught them the ways of Yahweh and much of what Kei, the great priest, taught him. Jabari continued to teach and train his family for many years until outside forces threatened his village and his family's way of life. Like other warriors within the village, Jabari chose to fight to defend his home. The warriors gathered their weapons and packed everything they needed. They said their goodbyes to their families and left for battle. As the warriors left, Jabari's son cried out for his father. He begged his father to let him fight in battle with him; however, his father refused. His father said to him, "My son, you are not ready," then kissed him on the forehead and left."

Suncomba stared in disbelief as he listened to Tungo tell the story of what happened to Jabari. His breathing became rapid, and his heart began to race. He was in awe, for the story sounded so familiar, like a dream he once lived, or a story he had heard before.

"After Jabari kissed his son, he told him to look after his mother while he was away. His son agreed. Jabari kissed and hugged Nema before racing down the road to catch up with the other warriors. He turned and waved to his family, not knowing if he would ever see them again." Tungo said as he looked out over the water.

Suncomba felt the pain and loneliness the little boy felt deep within his heart, for he too had lost his father to war.

"Tungo, what was the little boy's name?" Suncomba asked as his hands trembled.

"His name does not matter for he was but a child from a long-lost past," Tungo replied, as he peered down into the pool at the bottom of the waterfall in sadness.

Suncomba became calm, and his hands stopped trembling, for Tungo was right. The child's name was not significant. It had nothing to do with Suncomba. As he thought on what Tungo had said, Suncomba got up and walked back inside the cave. He sat down by the fire. The fire had grown dim, so he added more wood. Slowly the flames grew hotter.

Suncomba stared deep into the flames as they grew bigger and brighter. He could not stop thinking about Jabari and his son. It brought back painful memories of how he, himself, had once longed for his father. It broke him inside. Being the fierce defender that he was, Suncomba would never share that part of himself with anyone. Instead, he would bottle it up inside forever, or unleash it on detestable evil individuals.

After a while, Queen Jai'Diah joined Suncomba by the fireside. Though he was her protector, Suncomba was also her closest and dearest friend. Queen Jai'Diah knew that something was wrong. She saw that her friend was hurting. She sat down beside Suncomba, yet she did not say a word. Suncomba was thankful that she did not speak, because he did not feel like talking, so the two of them just stared into the fire, listening to the crackling sound of the burning wood.

Some time later, Tungo entered the cave carrying more firewood to help keep the fire going. After he sat the wood down in a pile, he sat down by the fire. He sat quietly for a few minutes but soon interrupted the silence as he began to hum a song. As he hummed, Suncomba and Queen Jai'Diah began to hum the same song. Suddenly Queen Jai'Diah stopped and looked at Tungo.

"How do you know this song?" she asked with a puzzled look upon her face.

"Yes, how do you know this song?" Suncomba asked as well.

Tungo continued to hum the song as tears streamed down his face.

"My father wrote this song for me; it is the only..." Suncomba said before being interrupted by Queen Jai'Diah.

"No, my father wrote this song for me." She cried, staring at Tungo.

Tungo continued humming the song a little longer, then stopped. He then looked up with a tear stain face at Queen Jai'Diah and Suncomba, who were both standing in front of him, awaiting an answer.

"Yes, you are right, this song was written for the both of you. Tungo answered.

"How do you know this?" Suncomba asked.

"Because I sang it to you both."

"My father wrote the song for me, and it was the most precious of the things I had to remember him by, and when I became a father, I added to it for my children."

"How is this possible?" Queen Jai'Diah asked.

"It cannot be; my father was killed in battle." Suncomba replied.

"I watched as my father was beaten and dragged down the road by our village Elders." Queen Jai'Diah said.

"They beat him to death for being a member of the Forbidden Tribe, the Fire Tribe."

"You lie!" Suncomba shouted. "This is not true. It is not possible."

"It is true," Tungo replied.

"But it cannot be." Queen Jai'Diah replied with her eyes wide from shock.

"How can it be?" she asked.

Suncomba stared at Tungo, waiting for an answer he knew Tungo did not have, yet Tungo stared into the blazing fire as he began to explain.

"Suncomba, my son, oh how I have missed you," Tungo said with tears in his eyes as he lifted his head to look upon Suncomba's face.

Taken back by Tungo's tears, Suncomba and Queen Jai'Diah sat back down near the fire, for Tungo was not a man that gave into emotions. Suncomba and Queen Jai'Diah listened as Tungo tried to explain what happened to him and why he had been absent from their lives for so many years.

Chapter 5
Flesh of My Flesh

The fire crackled and popped as Queen Jai'Diah and Suncomba sat quietly around the fire waiting for Tungo to begin speaking.

"Having people I love ripped from me, has been the most consistent thing in my life, even as a child. My father was a great warrior. He was the best in all the tribes. He trained me in the art of war at an early age. I became a great young warrior, but nothing like my father. My father loved my mother and I so much that when enemies threatened our village, he and other warriors from the village went out to meet them in battle. My father hugged me and kissed me on my forehead before he left. He told me to take care of my mother while he was away. After that day, I never saw my father again. The song I was humming is the most precious memory I have from him, for when I sing it, I hear his voice. I cared for my mother as I promised my father I would. She was lonely and sad without him. Over time, however, over time; she found peace in helping take care of the elderly and sick in our village. Even though she was heartbroken, she had so much love within her to give. My mother took the love she held for my father and shared it throughout our village and with me. I cared for her, and she cared for me. As I grew older, she urged me to leave the village in search of a better life. After she reassured me that she would be ok, I did what she asked. I traveled far until I came to the Village of Rojadaran. There I met the light of beauty, my sweet Penda."

Suncomba took a deep breath as if someone had crushed his heart in their hands. Tears filled his eyes until he could no longer hold them back. They began to stream down his cheeks, for Penda was his mother's name. But how could Tungo know this, unless all that he spoke of was true, Suncomba thought to himself. For he had never before spoken of his mother to anyone, not even his closest friend, Queen Jai'Diah.

Queen Jai'Diah moved over closer to Suncomba to comfort him. She had never seen her friend in such a vulnerable state. She was unsure of what to say or do. Tungo stopped talking, seeing how it was affecting Suncomba. Suncomba then lifted his head and looked at Tungo.

"My father's name was..." Suncomba said before he was interrupted by Tungo.

"Azekel," Tungo answered, "I know for that is my birth name."

Suncomba hesitated, and Tungo became quiet once more.

"Please continue," Suncomba said, "I want to know more. I need to know more."

Tungo took a deep breath, then continued.

"Penda was just as kind as she was beautiful. She was lovely in spirit, but she could be quite stubborn as well. Along with her beauty came rebellion. While most of the village women cooked, weaved baskets, cleaned, and took care of the household, Penda did that and more. She made bows, for she was a great bow hunter. Penda loved to hunt. She did not care what others thought of her. Penda loved her life and lived it the way she wanted. Often, she would stand out on the edge of a great cliff overlooking the plains early in the morning with her bow across her back. Her hair, braided in long braids swayed in the wind. She watched as the sun rose on the plains for it was her fav..."

"Favorite time to hunt, and it was the most amazing sight to behold." Suncomba interrupted.

"Yes, my mother was a skilled hunter. I remember her taking me to the cliff to see the sunrise, and she was right; it was the most amazing sight to behold." he said.

"I fell in love with everything about your mother, from the way she smiled to the way she held her bow. She was my first love. There was nothing I would have changed about her. She was everything I needed and more. She helped me heal the wound in my heart from the loss of my father. After we married, later, your mother gave birth to you, Suncomba. At that point, became a true man. I vowed to do everything in my power to protect you from the evil in this world, but I failed. As it happened when I was a child, it happened yet again. War came to our village. Many were killed, and many fled out of fear. Your mother wanted us to leave the village together. She knew of a place, a cave she had found on her last hunt. She said we should go there to be safe until the war was over. I kissed your mother and pleaded with her to take you to the cave without me, hoping to give you both a chance to get away unharmed. I stayed and fought alongside other warriors from our village. Just as fast as the enemy came, they left. I hurried as fast as I could to find you both, but before I made it to the cave, two of the surviving villagers found me. They were covered in blood. They told me that my wife had been captured and taken prisoner by our enemy. The villager did not remember seeing you with Penda, but I knew that she would die before she let anything terrible happen to you. After listening to the villagers, I began to track the enemy. I searched and searched and could not find either of you. Finally, I came to the place they called Keradon, where slaves are sold and shipped across the ocean or killed and buried in the earth. There, I was told that my wife was killed and buried, and my son sold across the ocean. Afterwards, I went to the place where my Penda was buried and wept. My world came to an end that day, for my only son had been sold and shipped to an unknown land, and my beloved Penda was no more. I was no more. I became but a reckless wretch, wondering to and fro throughout the land. I was a ghost, no longer body and soul for my soul had been snatched from me. I was misery to everyone who met me until I wandered into the small village of Cocoachee."

"Cocoachee?" Queen Jai'Diah said, with a surprised look upon her face. "That is my village, my home."

"Yes, I know," replied Tungo.

"It is where I met your mother. We were both in the darkest storms of our lives when our paths crossed. We had no will to live, yet we helped each other heal from our broken hearts. We became each other's strength. We learned to love again. It was beautiful and passionate. But it short-lived, for there were those who were not pleased with our union and newly found peace."

"I watched as the village Elders dragged my father down the road through our village!" Queen Jai'Diah shouted. "They beat my father to death!"

"Yes, my child, they dragged me out of the village and beat me to the point of death. However, after the Elders thought I was dead; they spit on me then returned to the village. I lay on the hot, dry earth baking under the heat of the sun. I laid there for what must have been hours, clinging to life. Later, I began to hear voices, but I could not see who was speaking to me. Two strangers came along and carried me off to an unknown place deep within the jungle. I kept slipping in and out of consciousness because of the pain. I did not know where I was. Wherever I was, over time, the people there nursed me back to health. After which, I began to train with an elite group of warriors. They were very few in numbers. Restored to health, both spiritually and naturally, I pledged my love and complete devotion to Yahweh. I had been gifted a second chance and granted a gift. I have been gifted with the power to guard those chosen for Yahweh's great works. We as chosen warriors, must use our gifts for good. My power is not my own, but it belongs to the Almighty One who dwells within me. When I took the oath and vowed to serve the Almighty One, I only had one request, to be with my family once again. I did not know that the one I was chosen to guard and protect was my daughter; in doing so, I am now reunited with my son as well. I am beyond grateful to Yahweh." Tungo said as he fell to his knees and began to worship Yahweh, the one true God. Tungo then wiped the tears from his eyes and looked up at his children.

"Because, I am bound by oath to the brotherhood, I cannot say how long I will be with you. However, I will be with you until your kingdom is secure, and you are sitting on the throne as the chosen ruler of Africa, with your brother standing beside you."

"Is that why you destroyed the creature that attacked me?" Queen Jai'Diah asked

"Yes," replied Tungo.

"I did not know that you were my daughter at that time. I did not know until you began to hum the song with me. But it all makes sense to me now. My father, your grandfather, was Jabari, the only child of Kaijo and Maneza, the rulers of the tribes of Fire and Ice. Jabari was the sole successor to all twelve tribes, being born with both Fire and Ice in his blood. His bloodline is the purest form. You both carry this blood within you, for you are flesh of my flesh. It is what binds you so closely. It is also what places you in harm's way. For there is a great power that lies within our bloodline. You both are chosen. We are chosen for it is no will of our own, but the will of him who lives within us. I am your father, and you are my children. I will help you, and with every breath I breathe, I will give my life for you."

It was quiet for a moment as everyone tried to process all that had been said. At that time, only the wood crackling in the fire could be heard. Moments later, Suncomba lifted his head and spoke.

"I believe what you say is true." He said. "I knew that some of the stories you told sounded familiar. I have never spoken of my mother to anyone, yet you knew her so well. She was just as you said. However, there is one thing that I must tell you. When the enemy captured my mother, she forced me to leave her. She told me to run away as far as I could. She said that my father would find me one day."

Suncomba eyes filled with tears, and they flowed down his cheeks like a river. Queen Jai'Diah grabbed him and held him close in her arms. They both wept together tears of joy, for they were reunited with their father.

Chapter 6
Rite of Passage

A moist, foul stench filled the air. Darkness surrounded him like an army from the depth of the pit. Loneliness was his only friend. Had this become his norm, Kanto wondered, as he found himself in yet another dungeon. It seemed as though no matter what he did, he could never escape his past. The former evil of his days always found a way to reach him. It clawed at him, trying to bring out the worst in him.

Kanto had tried so hard to mend his relationship with his stepdaughter, Queen Jai'Diah, and for what? He was still yet a prisoner. He was no longer her prisoner, but a prisoner all the same. It was no use. Things would never change for the good, in his favor. As he thought on these things, anger, and bitterness grew in Kanto's heart once more. As he stared out into the pit of darkness, he saw the grim face of the source of all of his misfortunes. He saw his father, Chief Abebe.

For in Kanto's eyes, it was his father who condemned him to a life of utter hell on earth. Sitting there on the floor of Zendor's dreary dungeon, swallowed up in heartache and rage, Kanto suffered the thoughts of how his father destroyed his life. He remembered the day he met Imani and fell madly in love with her. That memory was short-lived as it was interrupted by the memory of how Chief Abebe tore them apart. Chief Abebe hated Imani; she was worthless in his eyes.

He could not see past her lowly status. The wound in Kanto's heart ripped once more as he remembered pleading with his father for his blessing to marry Imani. That anger turned into pure rage as he thought on the trap his father set for him to separate him from his true love permanently. On the day Kanto left for his Rite of Passage, he had no idea that he would be separated from Imani for years to come. As he journeyed on his quest, Kanto passed every test set before him. He knew that his father would not allow him to marry Imani if he failed.

After learning that Kanto passed every test, Chief Abebe sent word that Kanto must complete one last test. He had to find the cave of the White Lion and bring back its skin. Kanto was furious, for it was an impossible task. It had never been done. Those who tried before him never returned home. However, Kanto loved Imani so much that he was willing to do anything to be with her again.

Kanto continued on his journey. He searched near and far for the cave of the White Lion but could not find it. One day while searching, Kanto grew tired and sat down near an enormous stone overlooking the valley. While sitting there, he lifted his head towards the heavens and prayed for strength and guidance. He was weary from traveling and longed desperately for his home. He longed for a life with Imani. It was her alone that kept him going.

Kanto prayed, then leaned back against the stone and fell asleep. He dreamt of a short old lady. The lady walked towards him with a cane in her hand. She then sat down beside Kanto. She began to talk with him. She was incredibly wise and humorous.

"Kanto, my son, why must you sit here in despair?" she asked.

"My heart weeps for my love, yet I cannot return to her," Kanto replied.

The woman laughed uncontrollably, and Kanto was vexed, his eyes filled with rage.

"Why do you sit and mock me?" Kanto asked as he stood to his feet, towering over the little old lady.

"Stop your soaking," the old woman replied as she took her cane and popped Kanto across the knees with it somewhat hard, causing him to fall to the ground in pain.

"Quiet your mind and calm your heart." She said. "There is much to learn here. This quest is far more important than your love for Imani. It is greater than anything your mind can comprehend at the moment. But you will soon learn much if you are willing."

"How is it that you know of Imani?"

"My son, I know many things; however, Imani is of little importance right now. You will return to Imani, but first, you must learn the nature of things to come. You must prepare your heart and spirit for those things which will come to pass."

"What things?"

"You have a significant role to play concerning the future of our great. You will endure heartache and pain. However, one day all that you are about to learn will come back to your remembrance when you need it the most. My son, you are sure to lose your way along this journey, but you shall find it again if you wish to do so."

"What do you mean, I will lose my way?"

"I cannot tell you all things, just know that you must hide all that you learn from this day forward in your heart. It will be a present help when you need it most."

Kanto listened carefully to what the little old woman said. The old woman then stood to her feet. Taking her cane into her hand, she pointed down into the valley.

"My son, the cave that you seek is beyond the edge of the valley. It lies within the darkest shadows and is only visible beneath the light of the moon. Beware my son for your journey does not end there. It has only just begun."

Kanto looked on in the direction in which the old woman pointed. The old woman then turned and looked into Kanto's eyes and said.

"It is time to wake up my son."

Kanto immediately opened his eyes. He jumped to his feet and quickly looked around for the old woman, yet he found her nowhere. As he turned around, he noticed the sun shining near the far edge of the valley. Kanto remembered what the old woman had said to him in the dream. Though he was unsure of whether her directions were accurate, it was all he had to go by, so he followed the old woman's advice. Kanto was excited. He knew if he hurried to the cave and finished his quest, he would pass his ultimate test and complete his Rite of Passage.

Kanto's heart was beating twice as fast as he took off running down into the valley. All he could think about was receiving his father's blessing to marry Imani. Oh, how he missed her. It will not be long before she is wrapped in my arms, Kanto thought to himself. Kanto ran as fast as his legs would take him. Although the cave was beyond the valley, it was still a far way off, for the valley was grand.

Kanto looked like nothing more than a speck on the valley floor in all its vastness. At some point, Kanto grew tired and began to walk. It was during this time that he crossed paths with a stranger traveling in the opposite direction. The stranger stopped Kanto.

"My brother, I am Azekel," the stranger said. "Have you seen warriors with slaves in tow during your travels across these lands? My wife and son were taken prisoners as they escaped the attack on our village. I have searched for them both day and night for so long that I have lost count of the days."

"I have not seen anyone in these lands. I, too, am in search of something and have not found it." Kanto answered.

"May you find what it is that you seek, brother," Azekel said.

"May you find your family and be at peace," Kanto replied.

The two men bowed to each other, then went their separate ways. After walking for a while, Kanto picked up the pace once more. He ran until the sun hid its face beneath the edge of the valley. Kanto stopped and gathered some wood to start a fire. The fire helped keep him safe from animals as well as warm at night. The valley floor was cold during the night. The winds that swept across the valley floor made it all the more biting.

Kanto gripped his sword in his hands beneath his robe. He snuggled close to the fire and stared up at the beautiful starlit sky until he drifted off to sleep. Kanto's sleep was sweet, for he dreamt of Imani. She stood before him smiling and waving at him, motioning for him to come to her. Kanto drew closer to her and took her hands in his, then kissed her softly on the lips. They then shared a long embrace. As he dreamt of the love of his life and his homeland, Kanto enjoyed a peaceful night's sleep. Little did he know that peace would be last long.

The next morning Kanto awoke refreshed and excited. He planned to make it to the cave of the White Lion by nightfall. He remembered what the old woman told him, "The cave is only visible beneath the light of the moon." Kanto gathered what few things he had and made his way to the cave of the Great White Lion. He traveled all day, stopping only for brief breaks along the way.

Finally, Kanto was within view of where the cave was said to lay. He approached the area where the entrance was sure to be, just as the sun disappeared beneath the valley floor. As the moon shined brightly in the sky, the entrance to the cave revealed itself. Glowing blue symbols appeared on the entranceway. Kanto ran his fingers across the symbols, which were engraved in what looked to be a massive stone wall.

As Kanto ran his fingers across the stone, it began to move. The stone wall slid open, just enough for Kanto to enter. He walked inside with haste, for he was ready to complete his quest and return to his village, and to Imani. Upon entering the cave, the stone wall slid close behind Kanto. He had no way out. As he slowly moved forward in the darkness, he heard a thunderous voice call out to him.

"Why have you come here?" The voice asked.

"I am Kan…" Kanto attempted to say.

"I know who you are, Kanto! I did not ask you who you are! I asked you why you have come here!"

"I seek the presence of the Great White Lion."

"No! You seek to destroy the White Lion! Is that not so?"

"Yes, it is so, for I must do so to earn my Rite of Passage; to marry my true love."

The voice laughed. It laughed so hard the ground trembled, and stones loosen from the cave walls.

"Your father, Chief Abebe, will never allow you to marry Imani. However, you are too blinded by love to see that. He lied to you! It was all a trap, yet you still cannot see that! Your father would rather sacrifice his only son to the White Lion rather than allow him to marry such a lowly common girl as Imani."

"Sacrifice, my father did not..."

"Yes, sacrifice! Do you truly believe you can defeat the White Lion?"

"Yes, I will! Tell me where to find him here. I will defeat him and drag his carcass back home to my father."

"I will show him to you."

Suddenly a soft brightness filled the cave and there standing before Kanto was the most gigantic lion Kanto had ever seen. It was pure white and the size of four grown elephants. It had piercing vibrant-green eyes. The lion stared down at Kanto, who stood trembling before it.

"Do you still wish to defeat me?" the lion asked.

Kanto stood speechless and stared in awe at the magnificent creature. It was unlike anything he had ever seen.

"Your mouth moves Kanto, yet you have no speech." The lion said as he stared back at Kanto.

"I heard stories about the Great White Lion, but I did not believe they were true, yet you stand before me. You are real, and you can speak."

"You stand before me trembling in fear, yet you do not run or hide. Why is that?"

"I could not raise my sword to slay you even if I so wished. I do not know why."

"I have heard many stories, yet none of them spoke of your ability to speak."

"You are one of two people who have ever been able to communicate with me."

"I was told that many have sought to find you; however, none ever returned home to their families. Why did you kill them?"

"Because they sought to take the life of Ya'alon."

"Who is Ya'alon?"

"I am Ya'alon."

"Will you kill me too?" Kanto asked.

"Do you yet wish to try to take my life?"

"No, but I will not receive my fathers' blessing to marry Imani if I do not kill you and take your carcass to him."

"Your father will never give you his blessing, as I said before. How can you not see that?"

Kanto lowered his head in disappointment.

"Kanto, a man that will place his child in harm's way, is not a true father. He is merely a selfish being, for he is no man at all."

"Though you come here for your selfish reason, you are truly here for much more, for you have much to learn Kanto. A war is coming, and you have to fulfill your duty. You have been chosen for a test far greater than this Rite of Passage."

"What test?" Kanto asked. "What war?"

"I do not understand."

Ya'alon, the Great White Lion, then turned around and walked to the far corner of the cave, which was now illuminating a soft blue glow from an unknown source. He sat down in the corner, and the earth quaked. The White Lion then looked at Kanto.

"Come sit with me," Ya'alon said.

Kanto hesitated at first. He then walked over to where Ya'alon sat, seeing that he had no intention of killing him, at least not yet. Kanto sat down in front of Ya'alon with his legs crossed. Kanto looked up at the lion. His head alone was the size of the enormous stone which Kanto had rested against days before. Kanto was captivated by the majesty of Ya'alon. He felt a deep connection to him. Fear departed from Kanto as he sat before the Great White Lion.

"You say that I will be tested beyond this, how is that?" Kanto asked.

"There is a war coming, and the outcome of this war depends on you and the decisions you make henceforth."

"Me, why me?" Kanto asked. "I am the only son of my father, yet I fear he will not allow me to lead the warriors of our village into battle. He is already displeased with my decision to marry Imani."

"Kanto, I fear that you do not understand. This war does not concern the fate of your tiny village alone. It is the ultimate battle of good and evil. The future of the world depends on you. You must make a decision; you must choose sides. Who will you serve?"

Kanto stood up and paced back and forth. He rubbed his hand across his head. He could not believe what Ya'alon had just spoken to him. Suddenly he stopped walking and looked again to Ya'alon.

"Who am I that such things are required of me?" he asked. "I am but the son of a chief. I am no king, prince, or General of War that these things might be accomplished. Who am I?"

"You are the one who has been called upon by the Most High. You are the one who must go forth and do his good works. You will face trials and pain that can utterly consume you. However, if you remember all that you learn here, you will prevail. Seeds of jealousy will attempt to grow within your heart. Kanto hold fast and do not let them take root. Rebuke them sharply so that His will may be done in your life. A child will come into your life."

"A child?" Kanto asked with a puzzled look upon his face.

"Quiet yourself and listen to the words which come forth from my mouth," Ya'alon scolded.

Kanto became silent and sat back down in front of Ya'alon.

"Yes, a child will come into your life, but not any child. This child is chosen to lead the people of Yahweh back to him. This child is chosen to rule over Africa and all twelve tribes. You will cover and protect this child from all those who wish to do her harm."

"The child is a girl?" Kanto interrupted. "No, that cannot be so, for only a man can rule with such power and authority."

"Quiet!" Ya'alon shouted, so loud that the earth quaked again.

Ya'alon's eyes appeared as fiery flames of fire as he stood to his feet.

"Who are you to say what manner of man can be called forth to do the will of Yahweh! You have no power here! Only Yahweh calls and grants anointing upon whom ever he will!"

Kanto trembled in fear. Seeing the fear upon Kanto's face, Ya'alon calmed himself and sat back down in the corner.

While yet trembling, Kanto asked, "How will I know this child?"

"You will know her when you see her. Remember what I say to you this day, for it will be of great importance to you during the test to come. Do not let jealousy and hatred take root within your heart. You will war within yourself; however, you must remember all that you learn here, for it will help you. Take heed and cover this child. Do no ill will towards this child. Teach her the ways of Yahweh and all that thou know of him. Guide her as she grows into her calling. Do not abandon her. Heed my warnings Kanto for there is much at stake."

Kanto bowed his head in agreement to all that Ya'alon had said to him. Kanto was nervous at first, but he asked Ya'alon anyway.

"What of my beloved Imani?" he asked. "I have not done as my father asked of me; therefore, I will not be allowed to marry my love."

"Do all that is required of you, Kanto, and it will be well with thee. If you do not do what is required of you, a curse ye place upon your own head."

Kanto smiled and nodded his head in agreement with the words spoken by Ya'alon. He then stood to his feet, bowed to

Ya'alon, and thanked him for all of his wisdom. He then turned and walked toward the entrance of the cave. When he reached the cave's entrance, Kanto found the stone wall shut up.

"Why does the door not open?" Kanto asked. "Because we are not done yet," Ya'alon replied. "There is still much more I must teach you, that is, if you are willing to learn."

Kanto lowered his head in disappointment once more; however, he knew, in order to do the task set before him, he had to be prepared. Kanto lifted his head. As he stared at the enormous stone wall, he took a deep breath and exhaled. He turned around and looked into Ya'alon's eyes.

"Yes, I am willing. Teach me."

Thereafter, Kanto abided with Ya'alon for many days. He learned much, from the history of the twelve tribes, to the nature of good and evil. Kanto grew in the understanding of Yahweh and his Will. He trained in warfare as well. After many days, the time came in which Kanto was ready to leave the covering of Ya'alon.

On that day, Ya'alon took the sword that Kanto brought with him to take Ya'alon's life and he breathed upon it. When he blew upon it, it was as flames of fire. The sword blazed with flames of blue fire. Ancient writing appeared on the blade of the sword. Ya'alon gave the sword back to Kanto. Kanto, no longer a man of fear, immediately took the flaming sword up his hand. As he held it in his hands, he looked up into Ya'alon's eyes.

"Thank you, my teacher and my friend. Let our bond be forever unbroken."

"Unbroken forever," Ya'alon replied as he bowed before Kanto. In doing so, the stone wall of the cave slid open.

Kanto turned and walked out of the cave beneath the light of the moon.

"Take heed to all that you have learned here so that it may be well with you," Ya'alon shouted out to his friend as he watched Kanto's silhouette disappear into the night.

After which, the entrance to the cave of the Great White Lion closed, sealing it shut.

Chapter 7
Dangers Seen & Unseen
A Storm Brews

The greaguls traveled to and fro throughout the land, searching to no end for Jai'Diah. Men by day and ferocious creatures by night, they never stopped looking for her. The greaguls had all but given up when they came to a small mining village near the Kingdom of the Mad King. There, as they walked the dirt road through the village, they overheard a man shouting. He was speaking ill will towards the source of all of his affliction. The greaguls stopped in their tracks to listen to the man.

"One day, I will have my revenge!" the man shouted. "Look at me! Though I cannot see, I know you see me! I feel your stares! I hear your every breath! I hear your murmuring, and I know that you look upon me in pity and disgust. Disgusted, you may be, but pity me not! Your most lovely one, the one of whom all speak highly, your most precious one, Jai'Diah, did this to me! It is because of her that I no longer have my sight! It is because of her that I slumber beside the road, begging! She will pay with her life for what she has done to me! I vow it this day!"

"Quiet, you fool!" a villager shouted as he passed by. "We have heard the truth spoken, yet not from your mouth! It is by fault of your own that your eyes were taken from you by Princess Jai'Diah's protector. We are tired of your rambling. You caused this misfortune upon yourself, so much so that your slave master would no longer have you! Shut up and stop torturing us with your presence!"

The blind man lifted his head to the sky, took a deep breath, then stretched forth his hands to the sky above.

"I tell you this day, I am Nebo, and as I live and breathe, I will destroy Jai'Diah, Suncomba, and all those whom they hold dear. I must not forget Keebuh and his lovely wife. I will become their worst fear. They will regret ever having betrayed me. Mark my words, it shall be done."

As they stared at Nebo, the villagers laughed. They mocked him, then left and went about their day. As Nebo stood with his head towards the sky, it began to rain. The rain flowed down from his face like a stream. Soon after, thunder roared, and lightning flashed all around. Nebo began to laugh hysterically. It was such a wicked laugh.

As the greaguls watched him from a distance, they decided amongst themselves to take Nebo to Zendor. After everyone hurried off, seeking shelter from the storm, the greaguls walked over to Nebo. They stood in front of him, staring at the dark hollow holes in Nebo's face, where his eyes once were. Their eyes then followed the path of the long deep scar across his chest. It was so deep it appeared as though the person who put it there was trying to brand Nebo's heart itself. It looked excruciating.

"Are you done staring?" Nebo asked. "I know that you are there."

"How did you know?" one of the greaguls asked.

"I can smell you, the both of you."

"What do you want? Have you come to mock me too?"

"No, we do not mock you." One of the greaguls replied. We want to know more about Jai'Diah. If what you speak of is true, how do you know her?"

"What I say is the truth! Jai'Diah was to be my wife, but out of jealousy, her friend attacked me." Nebo shouted.

"You lie to us; I can smell it on you." the other greagul said.

"He was her protector and her friend! He was jealous!"

"No, I do not think that was the case. He was protecting Jai'Diah from you." One of the greaguls said.

"You know nothing of what you speak!" Nebo shouted.

"We believe we know enough." One of the greaguls said as he looked off in the distance.

He watched as the sun disappeared beneath the earth.

"Are you still there?" Nebo asked. "Why do you not speak?"

"Yes, we are still here." one of the greaguls whispered in Nebo's ear just before he snatched Nebo up and flew off into the night sky with him.

The other greagul followed close behind him. His enormous wings pressed hard against the air. Nebo let out a horrific scream, for he no longer felt the earth beneath his feet. His arms and legs swung about as he was carried off into the night within the sharp talons of a greagul. Nebo had no idea what was going on around him as the greaguls flipped, turned, and soared through the sky in route to the Dark Mountains.

Once they arrived at the mountains, one greagul flew directly through the tower window into the throne room, while the other, perched in the window with Nebo in its talons. Nebo screamed for the greagul to let him go.

"What is this animal? Nebo shouted. "What are you? Turn me lose at once!"

The greagul immediately dropped Nebo onto the cold stone floor. The fall from the window was quite a drop, and Nebo landed with a loud thump. He screamed out in agony.

"You, miserable, wretched beast, look at what you have done to me!" Nebo shouted as he cupped his nose in his hand."

It hurt so bad. Nebo had broken his nose during the fall. As he shouted, he could taste his blood in his mouth as it flowed down from his nose. The warmth of it covered his lips and chin as it poured down like warm water from a hot spring.

"What are you that you can live as both man and beast?" Nebo asked. "You have claws for hands, yet you smell the same as before. Where have you brought me?"

The greagul jumped down from the window, and the floor shook beneath its feet. Nebo struggled to keep his balance as both creatures walked towards him. With every step the creatures took, Nebo's body trembled from their thunderous vibrations. He tried to remain upright. Finally, the greaguls stopped moving.

"What now?" Nebo asked. "Are you going to kill me because I spoke ill of your lovely Jai'Diah? Well, you better get on with it because I take none of it back! If I had it my way, she would already be dead! Go ahead; I do not fear you! Though you make thunder with your feet, I yet do not fear you!"

One greagul roared in Nebo's face, and the other growled as it lifted its talons to strike Nebo down.

"Well, what do we have here?" Zendor asked as he walked over to where the greaguls stood, dragging the train of his long black cloak behind him.

"Who is that?" asked Nebo as he turned toward the unknown voice.

"Master this human knows of Jai'Diah and wishes to destroy her. We thought he might be of great use to you."

"Of great use?" Nebo replied, "I belong to no one. I am no use to you because I will not serve you."

Zendor laughed.

"I will decide if you serve me or not. You belong to me now. I will decide if you are worth keeping or if I should kill you. Tell me this, why do you wish to harm Jai'Diah? What has she done to you that she might be destroyed?"

"What has she done?" Look at me! What do you mean, what has she done? She is the cause of this; this is by her doing!"

"Hmmm, so I see why you are upset. I would be too if I looked like you. Tell me how you came to know Jai'Diah?"

"She was a slave in my master's house. We were to be married but her friend and protector became jealous. He attacked me. Jai'Diah was hurt during the attack and blamed me for the attack. My master believed Jai'Diah over me; he chose a filthy slave girl over me! My master took away my sight, and for that, I will never forgive him."

Zendor walked closer to Nebo, and with his hand outstretched, he touched the deep branded scar on his chest.

"What happened here? How did you get this scar?"

"Jai'Diah's friend, Suncomba, left his mark on me. It is something to remember him by, and that, I most certainly, will do. I will have my revenge against them all if one I had my sight."

"Let me help you with that," Zendor whispered in Nebo's ear.

"It is impossible, how?" Nebo asked, for he was interested in Zendor's offer.

"For you to do, yes, it is an impossible task, but for me not so much. All you have to do is vow to serve me. Do my bidding, and you will have your sight. Betray me, and I will take much more than your sight; I will take your life."

"For my sight, I will serve you forever, master," Nebo replied.

"Great choice. Now that we have that out of the way. Tell me, how close was Jai'Diah with your former master?"

"She was loved deeply by Master Keebuh and Madam Shaya, so much so, they freed her and adopted her as their daughter. Jai'Diah loved them so much that even after she was free to leave, she yet remained with them for a while. She was educated by the best scholars, taught multiple languages, and trained in defense skills. It would be an honor to do as my new master so desire," Nebo said with a sly grin that shown through the now dried blood upon his face.

Zendor looked up at his greaguls and pointed his finger at one of them and said.

"You, take two more greaguls with you to gather Master Keebuh and his wife. Bring them back here to me at once."

"Yes, master," the greagul replied.

The greagul then left to do as his master commanded. There was one greagul still standing by Nebo.

"And you," Zendor said as he pointed at the greagul beside Nebo. "Take him up and bring him to the Chamber of the Fallen."

The greagul immediately picked Nebo up and threw him over his shoulder.

"Put me down now!" Nebo shouted as he beat his fist against the greaguls back. "Where are you taking me?"

"To receive your sight, as you so requested." Zendor replied, "and so much more," he murmured under his breath."

As Zendor lead the way to the Chamber of the Fallen, he halted and turned to Nebo.

"Oh, by the way, what is your name?" he asked as he tapped one of his long grungy fingernails against Nebo's forehead.

"My name is Nebo, and do not forget it," Nebo replied in a stern voice, breathing heavily.

"Hmmm, I like it. I must say, it does have a nice ring to it." A most unforgettable name it shall be." Zendor said as he turned around and continued to lead the way to the Chamber of the Fallen.

Chapter 8
Kanto Vs Kanto

anto still carried anger towards his father within his heart. As he stared out into the darkness all around him, Kanto thought back once again on his past. He thought back to when he returned home to Cocoachee after his Rite of Passage and the quest for the White Lion. Thinking back to the day he returned to his father's house, Kanto clenched his fist tightly in the dark. Returning to his father's house was the beginning of Kanto's downfall. It was at that point when he disregarded everything he learned from Ya'alon, the Great White Lion.

Kanto could not control his emotions, and they got the best of him. He quickly departed from the path which he had been chosen to follow. When Kanto returned to Cocoachee, he immediately went to his father's compound. Chief Abebe was bald now, and his grey and black beard was braided and wrapped tightly with bright green threads. It was formed into a neat little bun below his chin. Chief Abebe was shocked to see that his only son had returned home.

Kanto stood before his father with a puzzled look on his face. He did not understand why his father appeared distraught. Kanto had been away for an awfully long time, yet his father did not embrace him. His presence surprised Chief Abebe. Kanto looked as though he had not aged at all. After gazing upon his son's face in disbelief, Chief Abebe finally spoke.

"How is it that you are here standing before me?" He asked as he walked around Kanto, examining him as if to see if he was a spirit before him.

"I have completed my Rite of Passage father, and yet this is how you greet me, as though you never expected me to pass the test," Kanto replied. "Father, I stand before you this day because I passed the test you planned for me to fail."

"I did no such thing."

"Yes, you did. Father, you knew that no one ever journeyed to the cave of the White Lion and lived to tell their story. Nevertheless, you sent me, your only son in search of this creature!"

"It was just a test in which you failed miserably; I must say!"

"You sent me there because I passed every test you set before me! You knew you would not keep your promise to me and give me your blessing to marry Imani!" Kanto shouted.

"You would have me allow my only son, to marry a worthless common girl! I will not have it to be so. My son, the future chief, marry a common girl? It will not be so, for I would rather give you as an offering to that beast the White Lion than allow you to disgrace our family name, my name! It will not be so!" Chief Abebe yelled.

Kanto stared at his father. His eyes ablaze, and his chest moving up and down rapidly. Rage flooded him.

"You say you passed all the tests set before you, yet I do not see the head of the White Lion before me. You lie! You have not passed the test; therefore, you have not completed your Rite of Passage. I will not give you my blessing to marry Imani!"

"I journeyed to the cave of the White Lion, only to find out that he was not my enemy; therefore, I could not slay him."

"You are lying. If you had even looked upon the White Lion, you would not be standing before me now."

"I sat before the White Lion many days and nights learning much. His knowledge reaches beyond the unknown."

Chief Abebe laughed uncontrollably.

"I will not give you my blessing, for you failed your quest."

"I no longer seek nor require your blessing. I will marry Imani because I love her."

Chief Abebe became furious, and he would not see it come to pass.

"If you marry this woman, you are no longer my son!" Chief Abebe shouted.

"I do not need, nor do I want anything from you. All that you have which you would give to me, I cast off. I want nothing to do with you."

"If you do this thing, you will never be chief of this village!"

"I do not wish to be chief. It means nothing to me at all. I only wish to marry the one I love."

Chief Abebe laughed. Kanto looked at his father with a confused look upon his face.

"Things are no longer as they once were. You will see." Chief Abebe replied as he continued laughing.

Chief Abebe then turned and walked away while laughing. Kanto stood there, confound by what his father had said as he watched him walk away. Kanto wondered what his father meant. His father stopped walking, then turned and looked at Kanto. With a wicked grin unto his face, he said.

"Do not worry, my son; you will return unto me; of that, I am certain."

Kanto glared at his father. Oh, how he wished to destroy him, but he could not. Although Chief Abebe vexed Kanto's spirit, he was still his father, and he could not find the strength within to do him harm. Kanto knew that more was hidden behind his father's wicked grin. He knew something was not right.

"What have you done?" Kanto shouted at his father.

"It is not I who have done anything." His father replied with a smile. "I am not the one you should seek this answer from."

Kanto turned and stormed out of his father's compound, kicking over a wooden stool as he left. His heart throbbed in his chest, and his stomach twisted in nervousness. He thought of what his father had just said to him. What did it mean when he said, "things are no longer as they once were"? This troubled Kanto as he walked down the dusty dirt road towards the village center.

As he made his way down the road, people came out to greet him. Many knew who he was. The villagers looked upon him in amazement, for he was still youthful in looks and handsome, not like other warriors who went on a long dangerous quest. Those warriors were broken, and their youth had departed from them. It appeared as though Kanto's quest had been kind to him. One of the older villagers asked him a question.

"Why has it taken you so long to come home, son?"

"It has not been that long, only a few months, my old friend," Kanto replied with a smile.

"A few months," the old man replied with a bewildered look upon his face. "The other warriors who started the journey with you completed their quest and returned to us after a few months, but not you. My son, you have been away for over two years. Why is that?"

"Over two years, that cannot be right," Kanto replied in disbelief.

"It is indeed true, my friend."

More villagers gathered around Kanto, and the old man got lost in the crowd. "Two years, that is impossible," Kanto thought to himself as he looked for the old man. How could this be? Kanto grew anxious. If it was true that he had been away for over two years, what had become of his love, what became of Imani? What happened while he was away? Was Imani yet alive?

Kanto's heart longed for her to know that she lived. It did not matter to him how much time had passed. He still loved Imani and wanted to be with her, no matter what. Suddenly the villagers that surrounded him began to clear a path. As Kanto looked on before him, down the path stood Imani, the love of his life.

Tears filled Imani's eyes, and she became weak when she saw Kanto. She fell to her knees. Kanto quickly went to her side. As Kanto looked upon Imani's face, he saw that the love she had for him was still in her eyes. Oh, how he had missed her. He was ready to make her his wife. Nothing would ever come between them again.

Kanto embraced Imani, and they both cried tears of joy. The joy that had engulfed Kanto's heart faded when a little girl walked over to Imani and started tugging at her arm as she called out to her. That little girl was Jai'Diah, Imani's daughter. When Kanto met Jai'Diah it dawned on him what his father meant when he said, "things are no longer as they once were." This infuriated Kanto so; it was as though hot flowing lava coursed through his veins. Later, Kanto returned to his father's compound. He stormed through the gate. Upon entering, Chief Abebe greeted him.

"Are things as they were?" Chief Abebe asked as he laughed at his son's misfortune.

Before he knew it, Kanto lunged at his father, threw him to the ground and began choking him.

"No father would ever do this to a child he loves, no father!" Kanto shouted with his hands around his father's neck.

"What are you going to do, kill me, your father?"

Tears filled Kanto's eyes.

"You did this to me. You have taken everything from me! You are evil! Although I carry your blood in my veins, I am not like you."

Immediately Kanto saw the face of the White Lion before him.

"Calm your spirit," Ya'alon's voice whispered to him.

Kanto closed his eyes and took a deep breath.

"I will never be like you." He said as he slowly removed his hands from around his father's neck.

He quickly stood upright, then turned and walked away.

"You say you will never be like me, but you are like me. I made you! I am your father."

Kanto stopped and turned back towards his father.

"You may have created me, but you will never be my father. Fathers do not provoke their children to wrath. As of this day and from henceforth, I wash my hands of you forever." Kanto said, then, turned around and walked out the gate of his father's compound, never to return.

As Kanto walked down the road, he heard the voice of Ya'alon speaking to him, reminding him of his calling. Kanto dismissed all that Ya'alon said to him. He cared no more of his calling. Heartache consumed him as he walked down to the river's edge. He then took his sword, which Ya'alon blessed with fire, and threw it into the deepest part of the river. Ya'alon came to Kanto once more. He shone brightly before him.

"Why have you done this?" Ya'alon asked.

"I cannot do what you have asked of me," Kanto replied.

"You must, for you are all the child has; you are her protector."

"I fear I cannot. My heart cannot bear it, for I now know that the child you speak of is Jai'Diah, Imani's daughter. She is not mine. How can I love and protect the seed of another man? I cannot, for the task is too great, and I am unfit for such a task. It is better for her not to know me."

"No, you need her, and she needs you. You must learn to control your emotions. Your calling is greater than you, just as Jai'Diah's calling is greater than her. You must protect and guide her; it is your duty. If you do not, nothing good will come of your life. If you try, you will have help when you need it most; however, if you fail to fulfill your duties as her teacher and protector, you will not prosper until you do that which you are called to do."

"Why must this be required of me?" Kanto asked as he looked down at the water.

"Because there is greatness in you, Kanto. You have a good heart, however, you must learn to control your emotions. You must remember all that you have learned, all that I have taught you. Remember what is to come will mean life or death for your village and your country. Choose your decision wisely, Kanto."

"I threw the sword in the river. I cannot retrieve it now."

"I know I watched. Do not concern yourself with the sword, for it will come back to you when you are worthy of it once more. Until then, lead and guide Jai'Diah in the ways of Yahweh. Prepare her as well as yourself for that which is to come."

Immediately, a bright light flashed inside of the dungeon. What happened? Kanto thought to himself. Was he reminiscing, or had Ya'alon really visited him in the dungeon? Kanto was confused. He remembered thinking about his father, suddenly, he heard Ya'alon's voice, and a light flashed before him. What was happening?

As Kanto thought on these things, the door to the dungeon swung open. There in the doorway stood an enormous ugly vile beast, a greagul. The greagul made its way to Kanto, with the ground shaking beneath its feet as it stomped forward. It came to a point and stopped in front of Kanto, hovering over him. It was hard for Kanto to see the creature in the dark dungeon, but he knew it was there. Kanto smelled a terrible odor. The stench of rotting flesh upon its breath was sickening. With every breathe the greagul exhaled, the horrid smell burned in Kanto's nostrils.

"Get up, slave!" the greagul shouted in a terrifying voice.

Though the beast was something to fear, Kanto did not fear it. He did not move from his spot on the filthy dungeon floor. Kanto just sat there in silence, which angered the greagul. It let out a mighty roar, then kicked Kanto over on his side. Kanto just laid there in silence. He did not fight back. He was tired of fighting. He was tired of trying, for he had been fighting for many years. The dark war of good versus evil had been his life's story, and it had consumed him.

"I said get up now!" the greagul roared as he kicked Kanto once more so hard that Kanto flew across the floor, slamming his back against the stone wall."

Kanto grunted as he lay there in pain, clenching his side. Bloody and bruised, Kanto still did not get up from the floor. He thought to himself as he lay there in pain.

"It is better for me to die here, for there is no hope for me. I have failed all those who have ever loved me, especially Jai'Diah. I have no one. It is better for all that I die here."

As Kanto thought of this, a single tear fell from his eye. Kanto closed his eyes and asked Yahweh forgiveness. When he opened his eyes, he heard the greagul rushing towards him.

"Get up or die!" the greagul shouted.

Immediately Kanto saw Ya'alon face in the pit of darkness.

"You are not forgotten, my son. Ya'alon said. "Stand up now!"

Suddenly, Kanto regained his strength and quickly stood to his feet.

"You are not forgotten. Remember, all that you have been taught. Show yourself worthy."

Seeing that Kanto was now up from the floor, the greagul did not harm him any further. Instead, he grabbed him by the arms and dragged him out of the dungeon. Kanto robe ripped, and he suffered many scrapes as the greagul dragged him up the stairs to Zendor's throne room. Once inside the throne room, the greagul slung Kanto across the floor, causing him to land in front of Zendor's throne. Zendor looked down at Kanto's beat-up body.

"Now, now that is no way to treat our special guest," Zendor said with a slight grin upon his face.

"Come now, stand to your feet so that I might have a better look at you. You have been in the darkness for quite some time since our last visit. Do you know why I called you before me today?"

"No, I do not," Kanto replied as he held one hand against his side.

He was still in some pain from the greagul's kicks.

"Kanto, our time draws near, and the days are upon us in which we will have our revenge against Jai'Diah." Zendor said as he twirled his dagger between his long slender pale fingers.

"I am afraid the revenge you seek will not be easily taken," Kanto replied, still yet gripping his side in pain.

"You doubt my powers!" Zendor shouted as he jumped up from his throne.

Zendor then took his dagger and threw it toward Kanto's head. It was so close it sliced the top of Kanto's ear before piercing the stone wall behind his head. Kanto turned and looked at the dagger in the wall, then reached up and touched his ear as he turned back around to face Zendor. Kanto looked at Zendor, then looked down at his hand, which was covered in his blood.

As blood streamed down the side of his neck, Kanto stared into Zendor's eyes. He made a tight fist with his blood-covered hand. As he stood staring at Zendor, his warm blood dripped down onto the cold, hard stone beneath his feet.

"Ahhh, calm yourself, Kanto," Zendor said. "It is but a flesh wound. No need for more of your blood to be spilled this day. We both have need of each other. Remember, I can help you get your revenge on Jai'Diah and you can help me build an empire. You can rule beside me and have the life you only dreamed of living."

As Zendor spoke, Kanto slowly relaxed his fist. He became calm.

"There, there, now that is more like it. Greagul, bring a cloth for him and clean up this blood. Now that we have an understanding, let us move forward with our plan."

"What is your plan?" Kanto asked."

Zendor sat back down on his throne as he thought on Kanto's question. Meanwhile, the greagul returned and threw a filthy rag at Kanto's feet and walked away.

"I know!" Zendor answered. "I will have my greaguls find Jai'Diah and bring her to me, then I will make her reveal the Golden Book of Knowledge's power to me."

Kanto looked unimpressed.

"What is it?" Zendor asked. "Do you not like my plan?"

Kanto stood silently.

"Do not be afraid to speak. Tell me your thoughts."

"Forgive me, Zendor, for what I must say," Kanto replied.

"Go on, go on, say it." Zendor interrupted.

"Your greaguls have searched night and day, yet they still have not found Jai'Diah, and they will not find her, for this is not the way."

"What do you mean, not the way?" Zendor shouted.

"I will explain."

"Well, get on with it."

"Jai'Diah is wise beyond her years, and she genuinely loves her people. To find Jai'Diah, you must threaten those closest to her. To do that, you must take possession of her beloved kingdom. Jai'Diah's family is dead and her kingdom all but destroyed; therefore, she will want her revenge. If you take her kingdom, you will not have to worry about finding her, for she will find you. She will defend her people and come for you."

"Let her come, I will be ready for her," Zendor said in a most wicked voice.

Although Zendor liked the idea, Kanto knew that Jai'Diah was not who she once was. She was no longer that weak little girl, for he had witnessed Jai'Diah's transformation himself. Kanto knew that Jai'Diah was stronger and would fight for her kingdom, her people, and her throne.

"Zendor, do not make the mistake of underestimating her as I have done."

"I am not a fool like you. Look at me, look at all that I have created. I have amassed an army like no other. What do I have to fear of Jai'Diah? She is nothing. I will bring an end to her. I will crush all that she holds dear, and she will bow to me. She will reveal the power of the Golden Book to me, and she will be my slave."

"Jai'Diah will never bow to you no matter what you do to her. She will not reveal the power of the Golden Book to you. She is the Guardian of the Golden Book of Knowledge, chosen to lead the people back to Yahweh. She will not turn to the left nor the right, for she knows the path she must take and walk therein."

Zendor once again arose from his throne. He glared at Kanto with fire in his eyes and laughed wickedly.

"My dear Kanto," he said as he walked slowly down the steps from his throne, dragging the train of his cloak behind him. "I have a little surprise for our sweet Jai'Diah. Bring me the prisoners!" he shouted.

One of the greagul hurried off and later returned, dragging a woman and a man across the floor. It threw them at Zendor's feet. Kanto looked down at the man and woman. He immediately knew who they were. It was Master Keebuh and Madam Shaya. Kanto stared in disbelief as he looked upon their faces. Tears flowed from Madam Shaya's eyes as she clung to her husband. Master Keebuh then looked up at Kanto with hate in his eyes.

"Is this your doing?" He asked Kanto with such anger in his voice.

"No," Kanto replied, still in shock. "I had nothing to do with this!"

"You lie!" Madam Shaya shouted. "You have everything to do with this. It is because of your hatred for Jai'Diah that we are all here."

"I am a prisoner, just like both of you! I am here against my will!"

"You are no prisoner! You are working with him." Madam Shaya shouted as she pointed at Zendor. "You have always hated Jai'Diah, yet she loved you so much!"

What Madam Shaya said pricked Kanto's heart, for he knew it was true. After all the evil things he had done to Jai'Diah, she yet showed him unconditional love. Unable to bear the pain of the truth, Kanto walked over to Madam Shaya and shouted in her face.

"Quiet! I will hear no more from you, woman!"

"You will not speak to my wife in such a way!" Master Keebuh said as he rose to his feet.

Kanto immediately took the back of his hand and slapped Master Keebuh to the ground. Master Keebuh tried to lift himself from the floor.

"It would be wise of you to stay down," Kanto said as he stood over him.

As Master Keebuh tried once more to stand, he looked up to see the greaguls standing by Kanto's side. Master Keebuh stayed down, for he could not win against Kanto and the greaguls. Watching from his throne, Zendor clapped his hands. Everyone turned and looked at him with puzzled looks upon their faces.

"I knew you had it in you, Kanto. All of that beautiful hate in there, just waiting to be released." Zendor said as he poked Kanto in the chest with his dirty fingernail.

"A heart just as poisoned as mine, oh what a team we will make. Come now, Kanto, let us bring Jai'Diah's kingdom to an end. First, I must rid myself of a little pest. Come with me." Zendor said as he turned and walked away with Kanto by his side.

"Throw them back in the dungeon!" he shouted to the greaguls as he walked away."

"Kanto, I have much to share with you if you are ready."

"I am ready, let us go make war," Kanto said as they walked away, laughing wickedly, their laughter echoing throughout the mountain.

Meanwhile, far away in a tavern near the Mad Kings Kingdom, a farmer and his wife told a most horrific tale. They had journeyed from a small village afar off which lay near the Dark Mountains. The couple told the tale of a monstrous creature with enormous wings. They described in detail the terrible monster, from the length of its body to the scales of its wings. As they spoke, foreign ears listened.

Those who listened to the farmer and his wife were quiet as they took in everything that they heard. The expressions upon their faces were ghostly, as if all of the blood had been drained from them. Fear had gripped their hearts, holding on tightly, and refusing to let go.

"That was no creature you saw, no monster. It was nothing more than a large eagle that is all." a man said as he laughed.

"We know what we saw, and it was no eagle, for it was many times the size of any bird." The farmer said.

"One of its wings along was twice the size of you and me. That is like no eagle I have ever seen."

"You are just spreading tales of the creatures that were said to have attacked Monmuket, King Abdu's Kingdom. You have seen nothing of your own. You spread only that which you have heard."

"What attack on a kingdom? We know nothing of such an attack."

"Yes, you do. The creatures you described are the same ones described by the survivors of the attack on Monmuket. You have heard the stories just as I have, and now you speak lies as if you were there amongst the battle."

"If these creatures attacked Monmuket, we must go to the king and warn him, for they will return. I fear there are many more of the creatures within the Dark Mountains. Something evil dwells there."

"How will you warn the king of Monmuket when he is already dead?" the man replied.

"Dead?" the farmer's wife asked with a look of terror upon her face.

"Yes, dead. The members of the royal family were killed, and no one is left to sit upon the throne."

"If you do not believe the creatures exist, then how do you know all of this?" the farmer asked.

"I know because as I was journeying through the lands, I came across a kingdom in ruins. I asked, what happened, and the survivors told me a most terrifying tale of monsters, warriors, shadows, and the death of their beloved king. You see, I never saw the creatures, so I do not believe they are real. I believe that King Abdu was betrayed by his warriors, and in an attempt to cover it up, they blamed it on some made-up beast."

"The survivors are not lying!" the farmer's wife shouted. "I have seen them, and we all have much to fear."

"You are correct." Another man said as he stood up from where he was sitting, cloaked in a long blue robe. "We all should be greatly afraid of what is to come. The creature you speak of is much more than a mere creature. It is both man and beast. As I traveled the road from my village, I too saw the beast. I watched as the beast soared through the sky. As it drew near to the earth, it landed upright, taking the form of a man, ahead on the road before me. Fear gripped me from the top of my head to the soles of my feet. I dashed into the woods, and there I remained, quiet until I felt it was safe to travel again."

The man turned and looked upon the face of the man that did not believe the creatures were real. He was sitting at a table, taking another sip of wine from his jug.

"I tell you this, if you do not believe nor harken to what is being said unto you, you are the only fool in this place. There is a war coming, and if you want to survive, then you better be ready to fight for your life."

Shook by what the man in the blue cloak had said, with unsteady hands, the man at the table sat his jug back down. Fear had overwhelmed him. The man in the blue cloak looked upon the faces of all who listened to him.

"A war is coming, be ready to fight." He said as he turned and walked out the door.

Two men cloaked in black from head to toe overheard everything that was said. They hurried out after the man cloaked in blue, in hopes of speaking with him, but he was already gone. The two looked all around but could not find him. It was like he had vanished in the air.

"We must go tell our brothers all that we have learned here today." One of the men said. "We must prepare. The Shadows must be ready, for war is coming."

Chapter 9
Order of The Twelve

———————✦———————

R unning hard, with their feet beating the ground before them, the Shadows raced back to warn their brothers. Their hearts pounded as sweat streamed down their faces. Like leopards, they ran through the thick jungle. Jumping over roots and leaping across creek beds, they raced on. War was coming, and they had to warn the others of the danger surrounding them. They continued until they reached the place in which the Shadows dwelled deep within the jungle.

There, in a green meadow surrounded by tall lush emerald trees, stood the most massive tree of them all. Leafy vines hung from it like long strands of rope swaying in the wind. The tree was so big that just one of its branches alone was the size of a typical tree. The tree was unique, for Yahweh blessed it. It served as the sanctuary for those called by him for his use.

Needless to say, it was an extraordinary tree, and only those chosen by Yahweh could see it. The chosen were the only ones who knew of its location. As the two Shadows approached the tree, they stretched forth their hands. Touching the center of the tree, they spoke these words, "Eelis, Elad, Ya'alon" as an ancient symbol with a fire breathing lion on it was revealed.

Suddenly the giant roots of the tree moved. They spread apart as the trunk of the tree opened like a doorway. A bright yellow hue illuminated from inside. The Shadows then stepped inside. After which, the opening in the tree closed behind them, and the tree vanished.

However, inside the Shadows followed a tunnel marked with symbols of the Holy Book engraved in gold upon the walls. The tunnel led to a vast cavern inside; it was breathtaking. A river of crystal-clear water flowed through the middle, and magnificent fruit trees grew on both sides of the river. The fruit trees were unique for fruit of every kind grew on them. The water was so clear that the Shadows could see the fish that swam beneath the surface.

As the Shadows continued, they came to a bend in the river where a beautiful waterfall flowed down a gigantic cliff protruding from the cave wall. There, on the ledge near the fall, sat Master Yishai with his legs crossed and his eyes closed. He was meditating. Before the Shadows had a chance to speak a word, Master Yishai spoke.

"You have come to tell me what you have learned, correct?" Master Yishai said with his eyes yet closed, and his legs still crossed.

"Yes, Master Yishai," the Shadows replied.

"It is as suspected, there are more of the creatures, yes?"

"Yes, Master," the Shadows replied, bowing their heads.

"Come, we must tell the others," Master Yishai said as he got up from the ledge, leaped down, flipping twice in the air before landing firmly on his feet.

He then led the way to the others. They walked along until they came to another opening in the cave. There sat more Shadows meditating.

"Come, gather yourselves. There is much to be done in such a short amount of time." Master Yishai said as he gathered the Shadows to him.

"Tell us all what you have learned," he said as he looked upon the two Shadows, which just returned from searching the country for information about the ruthless creatures.

"The creatures are many. They come from afar, from inside the Dark Mountains," one of the Shadows replied.

"We have to seek these creatures out and destroy..."

"Forgive me, Master Yishai," one of the Shadows interrupted, "but there is more. The creatures are shapeshifters. Man, by day and creature by night. They can take the form of any man."

The Shadows began to murmur amongst themselves.

"How do we defeat this type of enemy?" one of the Shadows asked.

"Quiet yourselves," Master Yishai said as he held out his hands over the Shadows to calm them down.

"Do not fear. Remember who you are and your training. Being that these creatures are shapeshifters confirms that they were created using witchcraft from the Fallen One. We must remember to use what we have been taught. If our spirits are pure, we will know an unclean spirit when it stands before us. Therefore, we must remain prayerful and pure from evil, so that we may know this evil when it stands before us as man. Purify your minds and your hearts so that you will know which spirits are of Yahweh and which are of the Fallen One. This battle is more than physical warfare; it is spiritual as well. Purify yourselves and rid your hearts and minds of all that go against the Word of Yahweh, so that when you fight, you are not easily defeated. When you battle against the Fallen One's army, you fight to win, for our God goes before his people, forever and always. Now you may continue your meditation. Remember to purify yourselves, mind, body, and soul." Master Yishai said, before turning and walking away.

"Excuse me, Master Yishai, there was a man near the Mad King's Kingdom who warned the people of the war that is coming. He wore a long blue hooded cloak. We went out to speak with him, although, before we could, he disappeared."

"It cannot be so." Master Yishai whispered under his breath. "If this is true, then the war has already begun. We must gather The Mantel together at once."

"How, Master? They are spread far throughout the land."

"Every Elder and Elect of the Mantel wears a unique ring made of ivory. In great times of need, the Elect must only touch the ring while thinking on those things which concern them, and the ring will begin to glow no matter where they are in the world. When this happens, all the Elect will know that it is time to return unto this place. The rings only glow if the time is at hand, and the need is great."

Master Yishai gripped his ring hand inside his other hand and closed his eyes. He began to think about all that the Shadows had told him. As he did so, his ring began to glow a bright white hue, which illuminated through his hands. It was so bright it caused Master Yishai to open his eyes. As he stared down at his glowing ring, both excitement and terror-filled him. He was excited because all the Elect of The Mantel were being called together after such a long time apart. However, dread flooded him because of the circumstance in which required their immediate presence.

Master Yishai held his glowing ring close to his heart. As the rings began of the Elect began to glow throughout the land, the rest of the Elders did the same. It was time to return home to The Mantel, for the need was exceedingly high. After receiving the sign, all the Elect begin to make their way back home to Hadriel, the Holy Place.

Meanwhile, in the Kingdom of Dekar, Zendor stood before the Mad King with Kanto by his side. Zendor turned and looked upon Kanto's face.

"Watch closely," he said with a wicked smile upon his face.

"Zendor, I see that you have brought an end to the Kingdom of Monmuket. I am most impressed. Come now and tell me how we should divide the kingdom now that it has been conquered." The Mad King said as he stepped down from his throne and walked towards Zendor.

The entire court of the Mad King awaited Zendor's answer. Kanto watched quietly. Once the Mad King was standing directly in front of him, Zendor stared the king in the eyes and said.

"I think we should divide it right down the middle just like this," Zendor said as he stabbed the Mad King with tremendous force in the center of his chest.

The Mad King grabbed at his chest, as his eye widened at the shock of Zendor's betrayal. Zendor then whispered in the Mad King's ear.

"How our parents ever thought you were a better fit to rule has always baffled me."

The Mad King's eyes widened more in fear as he clinched Zendor's robe, trying to stop himself from falling to the ground.

"Yes, it is me, brother," Zendor whispered as he stared into his brother's eyes, before releasing the Mad King's hold on him.

The Mad King then fell to the floor dead, before all the people of his court. Everyone started screaming, after which Zendor unleashed his greaguls upon them all. Kanto stood frozen in disbelief as chaos erupted all around him. The Mad King's guards fought back with all of their might, but the greaguls were far too strong. They overtook the guards with ease.

Kamau, who was an advisor to the Mad King, and a Shadow of The Mantel, fought to help those who could not defend themselves against the greaguls. Kamau had killed one once before, so he knew that the creatures could be destroyed. While fighting off the greaguls, Kamau saw that he was not alone, for there was one who was fighting alongside him. A woman, strong and powerful, wearing a purple hooded robe stood in the middle of the Mad King's court. With a single throw of her javelin through one of the greaguls' neck, the creature fell dead. She wounded two more in her fight.

Distracted by the woman, Kamau let his guard down. In doing so, a greagul quickly shapeshifted into a man, and crept up behind him with a dagger to kill him. Seeing this, the woman turned with her javelin.

"You will not touch my son!" she shouted as she threw the javelin as hard as she could, piercing the shapeshifter through its chest and into the wall.

Kamau stood speechless, staring at the woman. He was shocked and perplexed by what she had said. Kamau then turned and looked back at the shapeshifter pierced against the wall. As life left its body, it turned back into its original form. In doing so, the weight of its monstrous size broke the javelin, and the greagul's body fell to the floor with a loud thump.

"We must leave." The woman said as she grabbed ahold of Kamau's hand and led him into an empty room.

"We must hurry, more will come looking for us." The woman said as she quickly moved a trunk that sat against a wall.

The woman in purple looked down at a deep hole in the floor, then jumped inside.

"Hurry, come on," she whispered as she reached out her hand for Kamau to come with her.

Kamau stood there thinking, but after hearing a loud commotion near the doorway, he jumped down the hole. After which the woman asked him to help her as she pulled the trunk back over the hole. They knelt there in the dark listening as the greaguls searched the room above them for survivors under Zendor's command. The woman in the purple robe pulled back the sleeve of her robe. She wrapped her hand around the bracelet on her wrist, then closed her eyes. The bracelet began to glow a soft white hue. It brought light to the darkness around them.

While this was happening, Kamau looked around to see where he was. There were clay walls on both sides of him and before him was a long tunnel that appeared to widen and deepen as far as his eyes could see.

"Follow me; we must be swift and quiet." The woman said as she led the way through the tunnel with Kamau following quietly behind her.

Back inside the Mad King's Palace, Kanto looked around in amazement at all the destruction Zendor had caused. He was at a loss for words.

"Do not worry; I do not have the same intentions for Jai'Diah," Zendor said. "The Mad King was of no use. He was worthless and unfit to rule his people. He deserved what I did to him. I have no desire to put an end to the common people of this place; be that as it may, as future world leader, I need servants. Therefore, I will let them remain, for now. Kanto stood yet in silence at Zendor's ruthlessness. After all, what a bore it would be ruling the world without people, only greaguls. I will spare them for now."

Zendor turned and looked as a greagul brought the general of the Mad King's army before him.

"I will allow you to live if you chose to serve me."

The general agreed, and Zendor conquered the Mad King's Kingdom.

"One down, many more to go," Zendor said as he turned and faced Kanto.

"Are you ready?" he asked him.

"Yes, I am ready," Kanto replied with a most wicked look in his eyes.

"Well, let us go pay your step-daughter, Princess Jai'Diah, a little visit, shall we?" Zendor said as he wiped the Mad King's blood from his dagger.

"Yes, we shall," Kanto answered facetiously

"But first, we must gather the gifts to take to her." Zendor said as he laughed the most wicked of laughs, and Kanto right along with him.

As Zendor and Kanto scattered the birds of the kingdom with their wicked hysteria, it was quite the opposite underground. Kamau was yet following silently behind the woman in purple. He kept thinking back to what she had said, or what he thought she had said.

"Could it be that this woman is my mother?" Kamau thought to himself.

Was this something he wished because he never knew his mother. Kamau knew that the woman instructed him to be quiet, but he could not hold it in any longer.

"Excuse me, did you say that I am your son when we were in the palace?" Kamau asked.

The woman in purple continued in silence.

"Did you hear me?"

The woman continued without saying a word. Kamau quickly cut in front of her blocking her way forward.

The woman then stopped and looked at Kamau, then looked away.

"I know that you hear me, why won't you answer me?" Kamau asked, as his voice grew louder.

The woman quickly turned and faced him.

"Yes, I am your mother, now calm your voice," she said as she walked around Kamau, continuing through the tunnel.

Kamau quickly caught up to her.

"How is that possible?" he whispered. "Where have you been all of this time?"

"I gave birth to you, and I have been watching over you all of your life. Although you did not know, I have been in the palace with you since you were but a baby. I brought you here."

"Why did you do that?"

"I was protecting you from the enemy?"

"How? The Mad King was a lunatic, and you brought me to his palace to live!"

"The best way to protect oneself from the enemy is to hide in plain sight; therefore, you are never perceived as a threat."

"Please pull back your hood so that I may see your face, the face of my mother."

The woman lifted her head and removed her hood. When she did so, Kamau fell up against the wall in disbelief.

"Penda?" he said as he looked upon the woman's face. "No, this cannot be, but you are just a servant in the palace."

"No, I only pretended as a servant to watch over you."

"You have always been with me, even as a child," Kamau said as a tear fell from his eye. "You cared for me when I was sick. You helped me heal when no one else could. You have always been in there, in the shadows. As a child, when my heart longed for a mother, I prayed for her to be as kind and loving as you were to me. My prayers were heard for it was you, my mother, who was with me all along."

"Why did you keep who you were a secret from me?" Kamau asked. "Why did I need to be protected?"

"My son, I have known since before you were born that a great war was coming and that you would play an important role in defending our people. Therefore the safest place for you was inside the enemy's camp. They would never suspect you there."

"But how did you know I would not side with the Mad King and become like him?"

"Because you are special, my son and Ya'alon assured me that you would be safe there. He told me to hide within the king's Palace as a servant. In doing so, I was able to protect you and watch you grow into an honorable young man in service to a despicable king. Yet, you remained pure, uncorrupted by the evil forces surrounding you. You care for the people and do what is necessary to help ensure their well-being."

"It has been most difficult serving under the king's rule."

"I know, son. Thankfully, the Mad King is no more; however, now we have a more deadly threat, Zendor and his creatures from the Dark Mountains. Ya'alon warned of this."

"Who is Ya'alon?" Kamau asked.

"Come now; we must hurry. I will tell you along the way."

Penda told Kamau all that had happened to her before arriving at the Mad King's Palace with him as a baby.

"Years ago, and months before you were born, enemy forces attacked our village. Your father, Azekel, decided to stay and fight for our homeland, however, he sent your brother and I away to hide in a cave. He said he would come find us when the battle was over."

"Wait, I have a brother?"

"Yes, however, I have not seen your brother since the day we left our village."

"What happened to him?"

"Before we made it to the cave, I was captured by the enemy. I fought back but was taken anyway. I forced

Suncomba to run away before he, too, was captured and placed in chains. The enemy tried to catch him, but he ran as fast as he could and got away. I remember telling him before he ran that his father would find him." Penda said as tears filled her eyes, but she quickly wiped them away.

"One evening, while my enemies were distracted, I was able to break free from the chains that bound me. I ran as long and as fast as I could in the night. I did not stop to rest much out of fear of the enemy, finding me again. I found myself lost in a great valley as I searched for my son and my husband. While searching, I became ill and fainted. I fell hard against the earth. I lay on the valley floor weak and in a deep sleep until an enormous lion came and picked me up with his teeth. I lay in the jaws of his mouth as he carried me off. I later awoke in a cave cradled in the arms of Ya'alon, the Great White Lion. I was terrified at first; however, I became calm. For he had a gentle spirit towards me. He reassured me that I was safe there, and no one would harm me. Ya'alon told me that I had to stay in the cave until my child was born and that he would keep us safe from harm."

"Everything you need will be provided," he said.

"I asked him what child because I did not know that I was with child at that time. Ya'alon said, that was the reason I became sick and fainted in the valley."

Penda grew quiet as she thought back to her time in the cave. Her eyes filled with tears once more. Kamau did not pressure her to continue because he knew that it tugged at her heart. He decided not to press the matter any further at that time. Penda walked on in silence as she remembered Ya'alon and her life in the cave. She thought back to when Ya'alon told her she was with child. She could hear him so clearly as if he were in front of her at that very moment.

"You are with child." He said.

"How do you know this?" Penda asked.

"Because I do. You are safe here."

"I must go. I must find my son."

"Suncomba will be ok."

"How do you know his name?" Penda shouted, with tears in her eyes. "He needs me; he's all alone!"

"Your son will find you when the time is right. Now you must focus on yourself and all that you learn here." The Great White Lion said calmly.

"No! I must go to my son now!" Penda shouted as she jumped to her feet and ran to the cave's entrance.

She found the entrance sealed shut. She beat her fist against the stone wall that blocked the entrance.

"Open it! Please open it!"

"It is of no use, for I am not the one who opens and shuts the door. For the door will open at the appointed time when you have learned all that is required of you, only then will the door be opened."

Penda fell to her knees and wept for her son. She feared he was lost in the world without her to guide him. Ya'alon walked over to her and sat down beside her. Penda fell over onto Ya'alon's massive paws and wept. Ya'alon comforted her. As time passed, Penda learned to trust Ya'alon. She learned much from him.

When the day came for Penda to have her child, she gave birth to another son, who she named Kamau. After she recovered and was healthy enough to travel, Penda prepared to leave the cave of the Great White Lion. She was ready to continue searching for her eldest son Suncomba; however, Penda knew there was much to be done before she would find him. First, she had to complete the task required of her, which was difficult and time-consuming. Penda had to gain access to the Mad King's court. She had to plant a seed within the court, her baby Kamau.

It was a most difficult decision to make; however, to save the lives of both of her sons and countless others, it had to be done. Penda took Kamau up in her arms and hugged him tightly against her chest as she swaddled him against her in a cloth. At that present moment, Kamau was all that she had left, for she did not know the fate of Suncomba nor that of her husband, Azekel. Penda prayed that they were alive out there somewhere, together. She walked over to Ya'alon, stared deep into his eyes then hugged him, although he was far too large for her arms to wrap around him.

A single tear fell from one of Ya'alon's eyes and landed on Kamau's forehead. The spot on Kamau's forehead where the tear fell began to radiate a golden hue in the form of a starburst. After the golden hue disappeared, Kamau was left with what appeared to be a starburst shaped birthmark. The same starburst appeared in Ya'alon's forehead as well. The child began to giggle and smile.

Ya'alon looked upon baby Kamau's and said, "From this day forward, your name shall mean Lion Hide, for I have made an everlasting bond with you and your mother, now and always."

"Penda, reach your hand into my fur, near my heart."

Penda did as Ya'alon asked.

"Take what it is that you find."

Penda took something into her hand and brought it forth out of Ya'alon's fur. It was a gold and onyx bow with arrows made of ivory and beryl. Penda stood in awe of its beauty. Out of all the bows she had held in her hands, this one was the most magnificent.

"You will know when to use it. You will know when the time is right. It is a gift to you. Although there are only three arrows, you will never run out, for when one has served its' purpose, it will immediately return to you. This bow and arrows are a part of you now. They will always return unto you."

Penda gazed in amazement at her gift. She thanked Ya'alon once more; then, she left the cave with Kamau en route to the Mad King's Kingdom.

"Penda," Kamau said as he walked beside her.

She did not hear him, for she was yet thinking of her time in the cave of the Great White Lion.

"Penda," Kamau said once more as he touched her hand.

Startled, Penda jumped. She turned and fixed her eyes on Kamau. He was staring at her with a concerned look upon his face.

"What, what is it?" Penda asked.

"Are you ok?" Kamau asked. "You have been silent for quite some time now."

"How was it?"

"How was what?"

"Your time in the cave, how was it?"

"I struggled at first, for I missed my husband and my son; however, it got better with time as I prepared for your birth. You gave me a reason to go on, a reason to live when I had nothing left to live for. You saved me, and you were born in a cave, the cave of the Great White Lion. You are special, Kamau. You share an everlasting bond with Ya'alon, the Great White Lion. The starburst on your forehead, Ya'alon also has it on his head. Only he knows the extent of your gift."

"Gift?" Kamau said with a confused look upon his face.

"Yes, my son, you have a gift, it will be revealed in due time."

"Son, I never stopped loving you. Everything I have done has been for your protection and that of your brother. Although I do not know where he is, I pray a covering of protection over him and your father."

"I am thankful that I now know my mother, although you were there all along. I pray that I get to meet my father and brother one day."

"Me too son, me too."

"Now, let us pick up the pace for there is much work ahead of us," Penda said as she raced through the tunnel.

Kamau followed quickly behind her. They traveled with haste, only stopping for short breaks to catch their breath. After racing through the tunnel, Penda and Kamau came to a place where writing appeared upon the tunnel walls. It was an ancient language written in gold, that illuminated with every new step they took through the tunnel. Kamau was in awe at the writing and symbols. It looked familiar.

"I know these symbols, this language." He said. "I know this; it is the sacred language of The Shadows, the Guardians of The Mantel."

"Where is this tunnel leading us?"

"Nowhere, for we are already here," Penda replied.

"Here, here where?" Kamau asked, confused.

"The Holy Place, Hadriel," where it all began. The sacred cave is where The Mantel and The Shadows meet."

As the writing on the walls lit their way, Penda and Kamau came to an opening in the cave. It was a breathtaking sight to behold. The ceiling of the cave was so high, Kamau thought it impossible for them to be underground, for this place was an entire world of its own. It was bright and full of life. As Kamau walked along admiring all that was around him, he heard the relaxing sound of water in the distance. As he drew near to the sound, he saw a crystal-clear river that weaved its way through the center of the cave.

Soon after, he heard the voices of people speaking nearby. Kamau and Penda followed the voices. There in the middle of the cave stood a small group of people in long robes. The people stopped talking then turned around to see who it was that came their way.

"Ahhh, it is our dear Penda," said an old man wearing a bright green robe.

"Hello, master," Penda replied as she bowed her head before the man.

"I see you have brought your son along with you.

Kamau, it is great to meet you finally."

"You called him master, that means that you are a Shadow," Kamau said as he looked upon Penda's face in disbelief.

"Yes, I am, and this is my trainer, my master, Master Yishai.

Kamau bowed his head to Master Yishai.

"Ahh, here comes someone you know quite well, Kamau." Master Yishai said as he smiled.

Kamau turned around to see who it was that came his way. It was his master, Master Bomani. Kamau immediately bowed his head to Master Bomani. Master Yishai then turned around and raised his hands in the air to get everyone's attention.

"Come now, everyone, let us gather. We have all been called together for an important task. Though there are only a few of us here now, the others Elects are on their way here now and will be here shortly. Everyone, I would have you meet

Kamau. He is already a Shadow, although this is his first time meeting you all in our home, where it all began. Kamau, we are your brothers and sisters, the Elders of The Mantel. Kamau looked on as those who were Elders walked over and stood beside Master Yishai. We are here because we have been called back to this place to build our defenses for war against the ruler of the Dark Mountains and his army of fallen creatures."

As Master Yishai spoke more of the Elders arrived. Master Yishai continued to share the plans for war with all who listened.

"We must be ready for we are not certain of Princess Jai'Diah's survival or our beloved Prince of Monmuket, Prince Nayari. If Princess Jai'Diah is no more…"

"She yet lives! If I live, she lives!" a voice shouted from a far corner of the cave. "Do not speak of her as though she is dead for, she is not! She is strong, and a survivor, I know she lives. I can feel it!"

Master Yishai looked on as six people cloaked in long hooded robes stepped into the light. Two wore royal blue robes, and four wore yellow robes.

"Who are you that you speak that which you are not certain?"

"It is I, and I only speak of the things I know to be true." Prince Nayari said as he removed the hood of his robe from his head as did those who were with him.

The Elders and The Shadows were at a loss for words. Their Prince was alive and well; in fact, he was better than well. He appeared much more robust. He now had long locs that hung down over his shoulders and draped down his royal blue robe. Beside him stood Binta, the old woman from the Kyro jungle, also in royal blue, Ta'nesse, Jai'Diah's mother, Imani, and her two sisters, Amaka, and Amari all dressed in yellow. Everyone stood in shock for the royal Family of Monmuket was alive.

"Forgive me, my Prince, I mean my King, for we thought you were no more." Master Yishai said as he bowed his head, as did everyone else.

"Please stand up; apologies are not needed. Let us prepare for war. We must be ready to help my love, your Queen Jai'Diah."

"Forgive me, my King, I mean no offense, but how do you know that Queen Jai'Diah is alive."

Everyone looked on, awaiting an answer from Prince Nayari.

"Queen Jai'Diah travels toward the Kingdom of Monmuket to confront the ruler of the Dark Mountains in battle as we speak. It has been revealed unto me. She travels with a Shadow, Tungo once called Azekel by all who know him, as well as her most trusted protector and friend Suncomba."

When Penda heard the names of those traveling with Queen Jai'Diah, she nearly fainted, but Kamau held her up.

"My husband, my son, they are alive," Penda whispered as she covered her mouth with her hands in utter disbelief.

"My father and brother are alive," Kamau said as a smile formed across his face.

"What is the matter?" Master Yishai asked as he watched Kamau help Penda keep her balance.

"She has learned that the love of her life and her firstborn son yet live. They are the ones who travel with Queen Jai'Diah." The old woman said as she looked at Penda and smiled. "Ya'alon said you would see them again, remember."

Penda cried tears of joy as she buried her head in Kamau's chest. Tears streamed down Kamau's cheeks as he held his mother tightly in his arms. After which they wiped away their tears and turned again towards King Nayari.

"My King, tell us, how did you all survive?" Master Yishai asked.

"We were taken to a secret location by two Shadows. There, Binta helped me heal and recover from my wound. She trained me and made me stronger. Ta'nesse, the Elder, then appeared and took Amaka, Amari, and Imani to another place where they trained and grew stronger as well. She helped unlock Amaka and Amari's gifts as they prepared for the war to come. Now that we are all here, let us plan our attack and take back our home."

"My King, there is one more coming, for I can feel his presence."

An old man with a long beard wearing a bright blue robe appeared.

"Master," Master Yishai said as everyone bowed except the Royal Family, for they knew not who he was.

"Muji, my brother, it is a blessing to see you again."

Master Yishai lifted his head and smiled.

"It is a blessing to see you as well." He replied.

"Who are you?" King Nayari asked as he looked at the man in the blue robe.

"I am Jabari, Ruler of all twelve tribes, son of Kaijo and Mazena rulers of the Tribes of Fire and Ice, born of both bloodlines. Keeper of the Dark Forest and the Cave of Mysteries, Father of Azekel, grandfather of Queen Jai'Diah, Suncomba, and Kamau; this is who I am."

King Nayari fell to his knees and bowed his head to Master Jabari.

"Forgive me; I did not know." He said.

"It is ok, my son, stand to your feet."

Imani was speechless. Her first husband was not dead. Queen Jai'Diah's father was alive and was traveling with her. How could this be, she thought to herself. She felt her legs weaken beneath her. On the other side of the cave, Penda stood in shock as well.

Penda's husband had moved on without her; she thought to herself. His daughter was Queen Jai'Diah. It was almost too much to bear. Imani knew that Azekel thought his first wife, Penda, had been killed and his son sold into slavery. Imani carried no ill will towards Azekel for she knew his heartbreak and how much he cherished Penda and Suncomba. Had he not thought them to be dead and lost to him, he would have never married Imani.

Although it was much to take in, Imani was not upset. She was happy that Azekel was reunited with Queen Jai'Diah. Soon he would have all of his family together. However, Penda was not sure how to feel about it. It was too much to think about; she walked away and took a moment to herself by the river. There, by the river, Penda sat and watched the fish beneath the surface. A tear fell from her eye. While Penda stood near the edge of the water Master Jabari discussed battle strategies with the rest of the Shadows and Elders.

Seeing Penda off to herself, Imani felt she needed to go to her. She walked over and stood next to Penda.

"Is it ok if I stand here beside you?" she asked.

"Yes, it is fine," Penda replied as she stared into the water.

"You know, I thought he would always wait for me," Penda said as tears filled her eyes.

"He waited for you until it nearly destroyed him. You see, he was told that you were dead and that your son, sold into slavery across the water."

"Dead, and sold into slavery?" Penda replied with such a sad look upon her face.

"I was captured, but I forced my son, Suncomba, to run away so he would not be captured as well. I did not know Azekel thought I was dead."

"He searched all over for you and Suncomba. When he found me, we both were broken and had all but given up. I, too, had lost the love of my life. Azekel and I became each other's strength. We helped each other heal. I know that had Azekel known you were still alive; he would have never stopped searching. He searched for Suncomba near the ocean were the slave traders shipped slaves across the water, however; he was told that he was too later, for his son was gone."

Penda cried as Imani told her these things. Imani walked over and stood closer to Penda; she placed her arms around her. Penda cried on Imani's shoulder.

"I am sorry, Penda, I am sorry," Imani whispered as tears flowed from her eyes.

Penda lifted her head and wiped the tears from her eyes.

"It is ok; it is not your fault. It appears that my son travels with his sister and my husband, with his daughter. Tell me, why are Azekel and Queen Jai'Diah not with you? Why are you not together?"

"Years ago, Azekel was dragged from our home in the village. The Village Elders stoned him for being a member of the Fire Tribe. Jai'Diah was a little girl at that time. I have not seen him since that day. I thought he was dead. I thought the Elders killed him. As for my daughter, Queen Jai'Diah, I have not seen her since the attack on our kingdom where she forced us to leave for safety as she went back to retrieve the Golden Book of Knowledge."

"You have been alone all this time, without Azekel?"

"As you have returned for Azekel, my first true love returned for me some time after the Village Elders beat and stoned Azekel. We were joined in union and had two daughters, Amaka and Amari." Imani answered as she turned and pointed towards Amaka and Amari.

Penda looked upon them and smiled.

"They are beautiful."

"Thank you."

"Where is your husband now?"

"He perished during the attack on the palace."

All of a sudden, the ground began to quake. It sounded as if there was a stampede underground. Everyone tried to steady themselves to keep their balance. The Shadows and Elders turned and looked to see what it was as they aimed their weapons. Out of nowhere appeared a humongous lion, black as night with piercing purple eyes. It was Harun, King Nayari's lion. As he approached King Nayari, Harun laid down at his feet, then stood back up and turned in the direction in which it came.

"Harun" King Nayari said as he tried to hug the mighty animal.

"I am afraid it is time, time for war. We must go now to Queen Jai'Diah in battle, for coverings only appear at their appointed time." Binta said.

"Yes, this is true," Jabari replied. "The time is now. Gather your weapons, for we must leave now. Our tribal armies are already in formation."

Meanwhile, back at the Dark Mountains after having killed the Mad King and taken his army and land, Zendor put his evil plan into motion. After sending the greaguls to gather the victims for his trap, Zendor called Kanto over to him.

"Kanto, come let me show you the surprise I have in store for our precious Jai'Diah."

Kanto walked over and stood beside Zendor as Zendor stared down a dark corridor.

"Nebo, come forth," Zendor shouted.

Soon after, the floor began to tremble with every step Nebo took out of the darkness. Once he was in full view, Kanto shuttered at what he saw.

"Do you think our beloved princess will bow to me now?" Zendor asked as he laughed wickedly.

"Who, what is it?" Kanto asked, yet trembling in fear.

A very tall man with red eyes stood before him. He appeared to be at least twelve feet tall. His arms were as big as branches from a Baobab tree. He bore a horrific scar across his chest. When Kanto looked upon his face, he saw that hell filled his eyes. There was no life from this world in Nebo's eyes, there was only terrible darkness there.

He was unlike any human Kanto had ever seen. Kanto stood paralyzed by what stood before him, for whatever it was, it was no longer a man, no longer human.

"My dear Kanto, meet Nebo. He once the lead guard of Master Keebuh's compound. He lost his sight because of our dear Jai'Diah and vowed to get his revenge. The scars you see were at the hands of Jai'Diah's protector, Suncomba, and our guest, Master, Keebuh. You see, after you abandoned Jai'Diah Master Keebuh and his wife, Madam Shaya, adopted her as their own. Master Keebuh treated her better than you did and protected her, as was your duty. In doing so, Master Keebuh took Nebo's eyes, and now Nebo wants his revenge. Oh, how wonderful, I have two people that our Jai'Diah loves without question, and you... well umm, not so much. You see Kanto; this is the trap that will draw Jai'Diah to me, bringing her within my grasp." Zendor said as he closed his fist."

"She will bow to me because she loves Master Keebuh and Madam Shaya. She will come for them to save them from Nebo, my most magnificent creation."

At that moment, the greaguls returned, dragging Master Keebuh and Madam Shaya behind them. Immediately Nebo rushed over to Master Keebuh, picked him up, and threw him against the wall. Madam Shaya screamed in hysteria as Nebo rushed towards her, for she was so afraid.

"Come now, that is enough for now," Zendor called out to Nebo.

Nebo turned and walked over to where Zendor stood. Zendor then touched Nebo's arm.

"My friend, you shall have your revenge as promised, be patient just a little while longer," Zendor said.

Madam Shaya crawled over to where her husband lay on the floor, groaning in pain. She tried to help him. As Master Keebuh stood to his feet, Zendor turned and looked at him.

"Master Keebuh, let me reintroduce you to an old friend of yours, Nebo, who was once your lead guard."

"It cannot be so." Master Keebuh replied, astonished. "It is impossible."

"You took his sight, but I gave it back. It is because of him that you are here, not Kanto. I thought it would be something you might want to know. He promised to help me, and I promised him revenge. Now it is time we make good on our promises."

Zendor turned to his greaguls.

"Shackle the prisoners and ready my army. We leave now. It is time for war. Oh, the games we play. Hmmm… prepare Brengum!" Zendor said as he marched down the dark corridor dragging the train of his robe behind him.

Chapter 10
Wrath of the Lion
"Vengeance is Mine"

H uffing and puffing with beads of sweat dripping from her face, Queen Jai'Diah awoke from a horrible dream about the war to come, only to find Elad, her lion standing over her. Alarmed, Queen Jai'Diah jumped back, pinning herself against the wall. She stared deep into Elad's ocean blue eyes. His silver coat flickered against the flames from the campfire.

"Elad, is that you?" Queen Jai'Diah asked as she slowly rose to her feet.

Awakened by the sound of Queen Jai'Diah's voice, Suncomba, who had fallen asleep near the fire, opened his eyes, and looked in the direction of Queen Jai'Diah's voice. When he saw the huge lion in the cave, he quickly jumped to his feet. Elad walked over to Queen Jai'Diah. He brushed up against her, then laid down at her feet. Queen Jai'Diah touched his head and smiled.

"How did you find me, my friend?" she asked as she smiled at him.

By this time, Tungo had awakened from the sound of someone talking. He stood to his feet and looked upon the lion in awe. Queen Jai'Diah knelt beside Elad and rubbed her hands across his mane. She hugged him and with her face against his.

"I have missed you so much," she whispered as tears of joy rolled down her cheeks.

"My Queen, although I am glad that you are now reunited with covering, his presence can only mean one thing," Tungo said as he looked upon Queen Jai'Diah's face. "The war has begun, and you are in grave danger. A covering must find its Guardian no matter where they are in the world. It will shield them in times of danger, such as war. I am afraid the war has begun, my Queen."

"I know for I saw it in my dream. I know what I must do. I must return to my kingdom for my people are in danger, as is the rest of the world. I must fight. We must fight. My enemy seeks to make my throne his. If I do not go, many will suffer because of me. I will not have innocent blood upon my hands. I am not afraid of the enemy, for I trust in Yahweh. He is on our side. Let us go now."

"My Queen, I go where you go, and I fight when you fight, yet we do not know the strength of our enemy's forces. We must gather an army to meet them." Suncomba replied.

"Brother, I have seen them all. They are mighty in numbers and strength, but they lack power, which can only be given by Yahweh. Our brothers and sisters are gathering to meet us, for I have witnessed it already. Although our people be few in numbers, they are mighty in power. Our enemy has legions of creatures like the one that attacked me. Yahweh has already given us the victory; nevertheless, we must walk in it. To defeat the enemy, we must not allow fear or doubt to enter our hearts, brother. I am not afraid, for what is it that man or creature can do to me that Yahweh is not able to deliver me from? We have the victory as long as we follow him and do as he command us. Fear not, my brother."

"I do not fear my Queen, for it is our enemy who should fear me," Suncomba said as he took up his sword and spear. "I trust your lead, my Queen."

Tungo, Suncomba, and Queen Jai'Diah gathered their weapons and supplies then left for the Kingdom of Monmuket. Elad led the way. They traveled days and nights until they reached the majestic Ahadi Hilltop that overlooked the Kingdom of Monmuket. As the three warriors stood on the hilltop, they gazed down at the kingdom. Queen Jai'Diah was rendered speechless. An all but desolate land lay before them. The kingdom looked deserted; only a few survivors could be spotted wandering from a distance.

It was far worse than Queen Jai'Diah had imagined. The enemy had terrorized the people and destroyed the Kingdom of Monmuket after she had escaped with the Golden Book of Knowledge. As she stood on Ahadi, Queen Jai'Diah saw the ruins of her palace, the place she once shared with her husband. Oh, how she missed him. She thought back to that terrible night when she lost those she held dear to her heart, everyone except Suncomba that is. He now stood by Queen Jai'Diah's side as her most trusted friend and as her brother. Suncomba was ready to defend all who suffered at the hands of their ruthless adversary, one who killed women and children, man, and beast.

As Queen Jai'Diah looked on, she thought of her mother and sisters. She began to weep. No more would she look upon their faces for they had been taken from her. Their love snatched from her without warning. Queen Jai'Diah's sorrow quickly turned to anger as she stared at the mass of ruin where the North Tower once stood. Her stepfather, Kanto, was no more. Although Queen Jai'Diah loved her mother and sisters, it was Kanto's love that she sought after the most.

However, just as they were growing closer, he was taken from her. She would never get to hug him and let him know face to face how much she loved him. She had longed to help him understand that she was never a threat to him and that she loved him unconditionally. No matter what, he would forever be blood of her blood.

A raging storm like never before brewed inside Queen Jai'Diah's heart as she thought of her stepfather. Queen Jai'Diah's hand tightened around her spear. Her breathing became rapid as fire consumed her from the inside out. Her eyes turned a stormy gray and green mixture. Her hands began to glow as well as her spear, a soft green hue.

"No longer will our people suffer for today; our enemy shall have his day. No longer will I shed tears, but the filthy blood of my enemies. Today our enemies will know that Yahweh goes before us." Queen Jai'Diah shouted as she stared down at her kingdom with immense rage in her eyes.

Suncomba took his sword from his sheath. With his sword in hand, he lifted his hands to the heavens, and Tungo lifted his sword along with him. In doing so, Suncomba lifted his head and began to pray.

"Yahweh, Father, our creator, author of all things from the beginning until the end, go before us this day. Be our defense against all that is wicked and corrupt. You command storms, and they obey you. You build up, and you tear down; even the wind obeys you. Yahweh, our strength, and our deliverer be with us now and forever. We have victory through you, and you alone."

As Suncomba prayed, behold, a booming sound came from the east. Queen Jai'Diah quickly turned and looked in the direction of the sound. There, in the distance a great army gathered towards them with banners held high above their heads. On the banners were the symbols of the twelve tribes. At once, there was a great horn from the west.

Queen Jai'Diah then turned towards the west, in the direction of the horn. And lo, there was an army more substantial than that of the east. As the army marched on, the booming sound of war drums throbbed in Queen Jai'Diah's ears. The drums were so loud she felt their vibrations in her chest. The army marched on. As they drew closer, Queen Jai'Diah saw that they too held up banners of the twelve tribes. Queen Jai'Diah spoke the names of each tribe as they marched forward.

"Jaiden, Lashon, Mano, Niri, Oshea, Jaida, Eelis, Eban, Daan, Jonathan, Sam, Guryon," Queen Jai'Diah said in a quiet voice

All the while this took place, Suncomba never stopped praying. He kept his eyes on the heavens. Queen Jai'Diah quickly turned back around and walked over to her brother. She stood next to him and lifted her hands to heaven. There standing on Ahadi, Tungo, Suncomba and Queen Jai'Diah cried out to Yahweh on one accord.

As they prayed, things began to happen around them. Thunder roared, and the sky darkened. Elad let out a mighty roar that shook the ground beneath them.

"Father, thank you for your covering. Thank you for you are a promise keeper, and great is your faithfulness towards us this day and forevermore. All the Glory belongs to you as we claim the victory in your great and mighty name, and it is so." Suncomba said as he lowered his hands.

Queen Jai'Diah and Tungo lowered their hands also. After which, they heard another roar, but it did not come from Elad. Elad, Queen Jai'Diah, Tungo, and Suncomba turned around in the direction of the sound. They all stood in amazement at the most beautiful of all the lions. Its coat was so white it shined like the brightest of stars. So much so it nearly blinded those who looked upon its countenance.

Although Queen Jai'Diah's covering, Elad, was significant in size and strength, he was merely a cub in comparison to Ya'alon, The Great White Lion.

"How is it that you are here?" Tungo asked. "For every covering has a Guardian, for this creature to be here, its Guardian must be here also."

Tungo looked about for Ya'alon's Guardian.

"Who are you?" Queen Jai'Diah asked as she slowly approached Ya'alon.

"I am Ya'alon, The Great White Lion," Ya'alon answered.

Queen Jai'Diah was alarmed. Although she had asked the question, she had not expected Ya'alon to answer her. Everyone stopped moving; even the warriors stopped beating their drums. They all stared in shock at The Great White Lion.

"I am Ya'alon, leader of all the coverings. Tungo, you are correct; all coverings have a Guardian; however, my Guardian is held up at the moment; therefore, I shall do his bidding. He will show himself in due time."

Ya'alon looked around at the armies.

"Yahweh has brought you back together, and he will not see you separated. When you go forth, fight as one people, and you will not be defeated." he shouted in a loud voice.

Immediately, there was a loud screeching sound from the Kingdom of Monmuket's ruins. Arose from the ashes and ruins of the palace a monstrous winged dragon. Upon its back sat a hooded man cloaked in darkness. As the dragon flew high in the sky, its massive wings beat against the air. Every time the dragon shrieked; its underbelly illuminated bright red. As the dragon drew near to Ahadi the twelve tribes stood in formation, ready to attack.

"So, what do we have here? "Zendor shouted from the back of his dragon, Brengum. "Is it our precious Jai'Diah, who has come out to meet me in battle? What an honor it must be for you to meet such a powerful ruler as myself. You even brought your little army out to greet me. Oh, how thoughtful of you. It would be my pleasure to rip them all to shreds, or you can come with me willingly, and no one else will be harmed." Zendor said as he held out his hand and motioned for Queen Jai'Diah to come with him.

"Come, my dear, this can all end now, just come with me."

"Never!" shouted Queen Jai'Diah as she took her spear up unto her hand.

In doing so, her spear began to glow once more. She threw it with all of her might. It whistled as it sliced through the air, piercing Brengum's thigh. The dragon became unsteady and screeched in pain. Zendor held onto the beast by the spikes on its back to keep from falling to the earth. After gathering his balance, Zendor looked down at Queen Jai'Diah and the twelve tribes.

"You have made a grave mistake." He said sternly, with a most wicked look in his eyes.

As he flew off in the direction of the palace, Zendor removed a ram's horn from inside his cloak. He placed it upon his lips and sounded an alarm so high that the battered gates to the Kingdom shook loose and fell to the ground. Zendor then looked back at Queen Jai'Diah.

"If it is a war you want, then it is a war you shall have." He shouted.

The ground began to quake, and as the earth split, it rolled like waves in the sea.

"Come forth, my children, today is your day! Kill them all except her!" Zendor shouted as he pointed his long pale finger at Queen Jai'Diah. "Bring her to me alive!"

The ground continued to tremble as an army of terrifying ill faced creatures marched from behind both sides of the Kingdom. Queen Jai'Diah looked on as more of them kept appearing in mighty numbers. It looked as though they were multiplying before her eyes. Some of the creatures had wings, and some did not. They were large vicious beast with monstrous size teeth; some even had fangs. The ones with wings had long pointed talons like sharp daggers. Those without wings had long piercing gray and black fingernails that could slice a man in half.

They were hideous creatures, abominations created to terrorize mankind, created by Zendor, servant of The Fallen

One himself. The ground in front of the kingdom which looked as though it had been burned, rumbled, and vibrated. Suddenly out of the ashes and soot arose fierce creatures more wicked than the others. They broke through the earth with such tremendous force that dirt and rock flew the air as though a volcano erupted. The creatures held gigantic spears in their hands, the length of two grown men. Their eyes, like fire from the pits of the underworld, struck fear in the hearts of the remaining survivors as they fled for safety.

Some of the warriors of the twelve tribes became fearful. Ya'alon sensed it, so he turned again to the tribes and let out a roar so powerful it shook everything around him, including Zendor's army of the wretched beast.

"Have you forgotten who it is, the God that you serve?" Ya'alon asked. "*Have you forgotten the one who goes before you, and who is a shield of defense behind and all around you? Have you forgotten the destroyer of pestilence, plagues, and diseases? Have you all but forgotten the one true God, Yahweh, the one who eradicates armies and breaks the backs of those who torment his people? Let us not forget our God, the one true God, Yahweh. For it is not he who has forgotten us, but we who have forgotten him. Let us not fear but always remember. Remember, our God, the God of deliverance. Our God who brings peace. Our most powerful Almighty God, who even the storm obeys. Remember who you are, the chosen ones, called by his man. Rise, rebuke all fears, and trust him, for he goes before us, Yahweh!"*

Ya'alon then roared to heavens and Elad along with him. The earth quaked once more, and all twelve tribes shouted their war cries, for fear had left them. Ya'alon commanded the tribes, and they took their positions. Elad knelt beside Queen Jai'Diah. As Queen Jai'Diah climbed onto the back of Elad, she heard a familiar voice call out to her.

"Queen Jai'Diah, may we join you?" voices called out together.

Queen Jai'Diah turned to see who it was that called upon her. When she looked, she was without words as she looked upon the faces of her beautiful sisters, Amaka and Amari. They were now mighty warriors with incredible gifts. Queen Jai'Diah ran over to her sisters and hugged them tightly. The three of them were so happy to see each other; however, there was no time to catch up, for they were going into battle at that moment. Queen Jai'Diah looked around at those who came with sisters.

"Who are they?" She asked

"They are some of the coverings of The Mantel, our teachers who have trained us in the art of war," Amaka replied.

"Forgive me, my Queen, but we must hurry, there are more pressing matters at hand," Ta'nesse said as she held her spears in her hands.

"Yes, you are right; let us go now."

Queen Jai'Diah climbed upon Elad's back. She then stretched forth her hand; in doing so, a sharp whistling sound was heard through the air as Queen Jai'Diah's spear came back to her, with pieces of Brengum's flesh still attached to it. She shook it off onto the ground, then turned and looked at her sisters. She asked one last question before charging into battle.

"Tell me, what of our mother?" She asked. "Does she yet live?"

"Yes, she is safe in Hadriel."

"Good," Queen Jai'Diah replied as she turned toward the twelve tribes and lifted her spear into the air.

The twelve tribes shouted wars cries as Ya'alon roared and led them into battle. As the tribes charged down the hill into battle, with Ya'alon and Elad in front, Queen Jai'Diah thought about her husband. She had not asked her sisters of his fate, for she had watched him fall at the enemy's hands with her own eyes. He forced her to leave him, to escape Zendor's wrath. The thought of it caused anger to consume her. Suddenly she stood upon Elad's back as they raced into battle.

With her spear in hand, Queen Jai'Diah and Elad tore through the army of greaguls. Queen Jai'Diah pierced their hearts. The onyx stone radiated a purple hue upon her neck. Being endowed with superhuman strength, she destroyed many of the unclean beasts. Taking an onyx dagger from her waistband, she jumped onto the back of one of the greaguls, and with a mighty cry, she severed the creature's head from its body. A power, unlike no other, flooded her body; in doing so, she was able to fight without growing tired. Her strength and power only intensified.

Queen Jai'Diah's sisters ravaged Zendor's army like two of the most terrible storms imaginable, uprooting everything in their path. Amaka, gifted with speed and the ability to paralyze and control her enemies at will. With one touch from her hand, greaguls turned against each other, destroying one another. The tribes slaughtered every greagul Amaka paralyzed. Amari, a master with the blade, and able to turn invisible, sliced her way through many of the creatures. The greaguls were utterly helpless against Amari's attacks, for they never saw her coming.

Ya'alon trampled the beast and brought many of them down under his feet. Once more, he let out a loud roar, in which blue flames came forth from his mouth. Everything in his wake perished. Soon after, some of the greaguls took to the skies. Seeing this, Tungo killed a greagul then let out a loud cry. After which, his eyes turned bright green. He removed his robe, and gigantic black and gold feathered wings spread open across his back. Tungo, with a sword in each hand, took to the skies, killing every greagul in sight.

After seeing Tungo reveal his true form, Ta'nesse joined him. Her purple and gray wings, flapping in the wind as she battled the hideous monsters. Binta transformed into a great eagle as she too fought Zendor's abominations. Her voice was that of a sonic shriek that annihilated every evil creature within her path. The Shadows, Elders, Guardians, and the twelve tribes fought the army with all the fight they had within them. While many more winged greaguls took to the skies, Jabari, removed his robe. Suddenly enormous black wings spread wide across his back and massive antlers crowned his head. Jabari the Keeper of the Dark Forest joined Tungo in the battle in the sky. With his mighty sword in hand he destroyed creatures in multitudes.

Penda, in her purple hooded robe, with her bow in hand, took aim at the dreadful creatures. She never missed a target. With every arrow she shot, multiple greaguls were killed. Penda's arrows were so powerful that they pierced through every creature in their path before returning to her. Penda's arms never tired. She remained calm in battle for hunting was what she did best.

Ya'alon, Elad, Queen Jai'Diah, Amaka, and Amari helped defend their ground forces from the creatures on the ground. Tungo, Binta, and Ta'nesse protected them from the air. While all of this was taking place, Zendor watched from a distance, on Brengum's back. He took his ram's horn upon his lips once more and sounded an alarm. When he did, all of the greaguls stopped in battle and turned toward him.

"Bring Queen Jai'Diah to me now!" Zendor shouted.

"Come along peacefully, my dear, or I will rip this one, limb by limb," he said as he pointed to a greagul, holding Madam Shaya within its talons.

Madam Shaya cried uncontrollably.

Queen Jai'Diah looked up at Madam Shaya then threw her spear to the ground. She would not see another person she loved taken because of her. As Queen Jai'Diah walked amid the army of greaguls, they parted way to allow her to pass. They growled and snarled as she walked between them. As she neared the ruins of the palace, Queen Jai'Diah looked up at Zendor, sitting high upon Brengum.

"Let her go free, and I will go with you peacefully, but you must not harm her."

"I will agree to that," Zendor replied, after which he turned to the greagul and told it to let Madam Shaya go free.

The greagul then lowered Madam Shaya to the ground, and she ran away to find safety. Zendor then had his greaguls try to escort Queen Jai'Diah to the rubble, which was once the palace; however, Ya'alon and Elad stood between the greaguls and Queen Jai'Diah. Queen Jai'Diah walked over and touched both Ya'alon and Elad on the face and said.

"It is ok; I will be ok. Be ready, for it is not over."

Ya'alon and Elad bowed their head to Queen Jai'Diah then moved out of the way. Escorted by the greaguls, Queen Jai'Diah then followed Zendor and Brengum into the palace ruins. Ya'alon and Elad watched from a distance, ready for whatever came next. As they watched, Harun came and stood with them. When Queen Jai'Diah turned and saw him, she stopped, gazed into his eyes, and smiled, before turning and walking away.

At that moment, she knew her husband; her one true love had survived Zendor's attack. She did not know where he was, but she knew he was near, Harun's presence confirmed it. Queen Jai'Diah walked along, stepping over rubble as she entered the palace. After this, a greagul snatched Queen Jai'Diah up in its talons at Zendor's command. Zendor, yet on his dragon, flew to the highest point of the palace that was yet standing. The greagul carrying Queen Jai'Diah followed after him.

Once there, the creature threw Queen Jai'Diah unto the stone floor of the balcony. She hit the floor hard. The pain of the fall shone on her face, yet she did not say a word. She struggled to her feet. As she did, Zendor swooped down on his dragon. Brengum crouched down in front of Queen Jai'Diah as his eyes glared into hers. Zendor climbed down from Brengum's back, turned, and faced Queen Jai'Diah.

"Whatever you want from me, I will not give it to you." Queen Jai'Diah said sharply.

Zendor then walked over to the balcony, took his ram's horn, and sounded an alarm, yet again. Immediately the greaguls attacked again; therefore, the war battle continued. The only reason the tribes halted their attacks was because of Queen Jai'Diah, to ensure her safe passage into the palace. Now that the tides of the war were uncertain, the tribes, Shadows, and the rest of Queen Jai'Diah's defenses returned to battle. Ya'alon stormed through a wall of greaguls ripping them apart with his ferocious jaws.

Elad roared so powerfully it sounded as a blaring horn. In doing so, a swell of massive sonic waves vibrated through the legions of greaguls surrounding him, causing the creatures to explode on contact. Harun took to the east of the palace, fighting with the tribes from the east. With his mighty paws, he clawed his way through the terrible beast, slinging them about like rags.

As the war raged on and the greaguls kept coming, Harun lifted his head to the sky. It began to rumble, and purple lightning flashed all about. Harun eyes turned a fierce purple. It looked as though a mighty storm was brewing in his eyes. Harun roared so loud that the sound stormed the heavens. All of a sudden, lightning bolts rained down from heaven, vaporizing the wicked creatures.

The ground quaked as the earth opened wide her mouth to swallow the fallen creatures down into the pit of The Fallen's Lair. Those with wings and those without were cast down and destroyed before Zendor's eyes. Queen Jai'Diah watched on in amazement at the power of Yahweh and the fearless strength of his people.

"What is this?" Zendor yelled as he looked out over the battle in utter disbelief.

"There will be no victory for you today." Queen Jai'Diah said as she looked at Zendor.

"We will see about that," Zendor said as he turned towards Queen Jai'Diah.

He walked over to her, staring her down, he shouted. "Bring me the prisoner!"

Out from the rubble, walked Kanto dressed in a long black robe with a silver and black band around his waist, which held a most impressive gemstone encrusted dagger. As he stepped out onto the balcony, Queen Jai'Diah saw that Kanto held Master Keebuh captive in chains. Queen Jai'Diah stood speechless. She did not believe what she was seeing. Her stepfather, Kanto, was alive.

"How is this possible?" Queen Jai'Diah asked as tears filled her eyes.

Kanto looked at her in a blank stare. He showed no emotion nor affection towards her. It was as though she meant nothing to him.

"Yes, here we are. Well, let me introduce you to my second in command, Kanto, or as you may prefer to call him, stepfather." Zendor said as he laughed hysterically.

"What, what are you doing with him?" Queen Jai'Diah asked Kanto, yet in shock.

"How could you?" she said with immense anger in her eyes.

Not saying a word, Kanto walked over and stood beside Zendor. He then threw Master Keebuh before Zendor's feet.

"Tell us the secrets to the Golden Book of Knowledge or Master Keebuh dies," Kanto demanded.

"I will not, for it is a power you cannot contain, nor will I allow you to manipulate its power for evil."

"You will tell me all that I desire, or I will kill him!"

"Nebo, come forth!" Zendor shouted.

That name sent chills down Queen Jai'Diah's spine, for she could never forget it. The one name that haunted her and gave her nightmares for years. He had returned. With every step Nebo took out of the darkness, the stones shook beneath their feet. Once in full view, Queen Jai'Diah saw that it was indeed him. He was enormous and evil than ever before. Queen Jai'Diah saw it in him.

"We meet again, Jai'Diah," Nebo said in a deep dark voice.

"Yes, but I am not the girl you once knew." Queen Jai'Diah replied as she glared at him.

"Tell me the secrets of the book, and it will all end here," Zendor said as he brought forth the Book of Knowledge from inside his robe.

"Do what you must, and I will do what I must. I will not help you. Look down there at my people. They are not afraid. I am not afraid."

"Then, I will destroy them all starting with him!" Zendor shouted as he pointed at Master Keebuh.

One of the greaguls stood over Master Keebuh and lifted its powerful claws to strike him down. As he brought down his arm to do so, Kamau appeared from nowhere and leaped onto the greagul's back. Taking his dagger, he drove it into the greagul's neck. While this took place, another greagul attacked Kamau from behind. All of a sudden Kamau was endowed with supernatural strength. He tore the greagul limb by limb. For each one he killed another took its place, but Kamau never grew tired. Gifted with unimaginable power, Kamau continued on.

Binta, soaring above, flew down and dropped King Nayari onto the balcony so that he might help Queen Jai'Diah. Queen Jai'Diah, who refused to help Zendor was now dangling in the air as Nebo held her up by her neck, choking her.

"Tell him all which he asks of you, or you along with your people, will perish," Nebo shouted as he tightened his grip around Queen Jai'Diah's neck.

"Let her go now!" King Nayari shouted.

"Look, your little king has come to save you," Nebo said as he dropped Queen Jai'Diah unto the floor of the balcony, then stormed over to King Nayari.

He took King Nayari up into his hands and threw him against the wall. He began walking over to where the king lay in immense pain, however; before he could finish King Nayari off, Suncomba blocked his way.

"This fight is not with him; it is with me. Let us finish this." Suncomba said as he removed his robe.

Holding an ax in one hand and a sword in the other, Suncomba stared fiercely into Nebo's eyes.

"Yes, let us finish this," Nebo said as he charged towards Suncomba.

Meanwhile, Queen Jai'Diah called out to King Nayari. After standing to his feet and steadying himself, she asked him to please get Master Keebuh to safety. King Nayari called for Binta, and she quickly came to his aid. She swooped down and picked Master Keebuh up and carried him off to a safe place beyond the battleground. King Nayari hurried back over to Queen Jai'Diah who was now standing before Zendor and Kanto once more. King Nayari took up his sword to strike Zendor, but Queen Jai'Diah stopped him.

"I will take care of this." She said as she turned to her husband, staring into his deep into his eyes.

She kissed him passionately then hugged him.

"How lovely," Zendor said facetiously. "Too bad this reunion will be short-lived."

"Brengum!" Zendor called out for his dragon, and immediately there was a loud shrieking sound above their heads.

Suncomba and Nebo continued to battle, as the wind beneath the wings of the monstrous dragon pressed against them. Suncomba quickly took his ax, as he ran, he slid between Nebo's legs. With a swift turn, he slices the back of Nebo's knees, causing him to fall to his knees, screaming in agony. Suncomba quickly flipped over Nebo's head, landing back in front of him. As he stared into Nebo's hellish hollowed-out eyes, he plunged his sword into his heart, through and through.

Suncomba pierced Nebo through the branding scar he had left on him before. Nebo's red blazing eyes turned dark like black coals as he fell over onto the floor. Nebo was dead.

"Now, it is finished," Suncomba said as he wiped Nebo's blood from his sword onto Nebo's clothes.

Suncomba turned his attention to the black scaley beast that hovered overhead. Brengum, Zendor's dragon, had its eyes on King Nayari. King Nayari took up Nebo's spear in his hand.

"Why this should be quite amusing," Zendor said as he watched King Nayari face Brengum.

King Nayari lunged his spear forward, piercing Brengum in the side, all while Suncomba jumped on the dragon's back. King Nayari then took a dagger from his waistband, placed it between his teeth, and leaped onto the dragon. Barely holding on by Brengum's spikes, King Nayari threw himself onto the dragon's back. He pulled himself up until he was able to grip Brengum by the horns. Suncomba stabbed the beast repeatedly in the side as King Nayari took the dagger from between his teeth and plunged it into Brengum's neck.

King Nayari and Suncomba wrestled with the creature. Brengum shrieked one last time as flames of scorching red fire exploded from his mouth. He began to fall to the earth, pulling down a portion of what was left of the palace wall along with him. Suncomba, King Nayari and Kamau, who was yet fighting a greagul, fell along with him.

"Are you still amused?" Queen Jai'Diah asked as she turned and looked back at Zendor, with a sly grin upon her face.

"Why do you yet smile, your love is no more, nor your protector. Who will help you now? You have no one. Everyone you love, and everyone who loved you is gone! You might as well join me." Zendor said as he extended his hand to Queen Jai'Diah.

"You are wrong; they are alive; they live through me. I am not alone. I have Yahweh on my side and the side of my people. I will never join you. I will prevail."

"You will not prevail, but you will die here and now!"

"Do what it is that you must do, for I know Yahweh is with me, even now."

"You poor defenseless fool, even your stepfather does not care about you! He hates you so much that he is willing to stand here and watch me kill you. Oh, what joy it brings him to watch you suffer at my hands!"

Zendor took his trusted dagger from his robe and raised it to strike Queen Jai'Diah down; just as he lowered his arm, Kanto threw himself in front of Queen Jai'Diah to save her life. In doing so, Kanto took upon himself the blade that was meant for his beloved Jai'Diah. Kanto cried out as a searing pain jolted his body.

"You treacherous fool, you traitor!" Zendor shouted as he glared at Kanto, whose back was to him.

"I trusted you, and you betrayed me!"

Kanto struggled to stand even as his blood streamed down his back. He took a deep breath, then reached over his shoulder and pulled the dagger from his back. He cried out for the pain was excruciating, after which he turned again to Zendor.

"You were wrong," He said, breathing heavily from the pain.

"She is not alone, and she will never be alone again."

Kanto gathered his strength and steadied himself. He then stretched forth his hand, as did Queen Jai'Diah. Suddenly a sharp whistling sound filled the air. Queen Jai'Diah's spear came back to her, as did Kanto's sword anointed by The Great

White Lion. Queen Jai'Diah's spear began to glow. Gripping his sword tightly in his hand, Kanto held it high.

"What is this?" Zendor said as he stared angrily at Kanto. "So, you think you can defeat me. Have you forgotten who I am?"

"No, I just remembered who I am."

"We know who you are, and we are here to send you to the underworld with your master, where you belong, you, and your abominations." Queen Jai'Diah said as she took her stance.

Zendor's eyes turned blazing red, and his hands began to glow as flames flickered from his fingers. Queen Jai'Diah lifted her spear as Zendor stretched forth his hand. She threw her spear towards Zendor, piercing him in the chest as he sent flames of fire upon Queen Jai'Diah's arm, searing her flesh. As she screamed in pain, Zendor pulled the spear from his chest. He laughed a most wicked laugh.

"Is that all you have?" Zendor asked. "It will take more than that to kill me."

"How much more?" Kanto asked as he spun around, raised his sword, and sliced off Zendor's hands.

Zendor screamed in agony.

"No man-made blade can kill me." Zendor cried. "What is this? Impossible!"

"This is no ordinary blade; it was anointed just for you," Kanto said as he severed Zendor's head from his body.

After which Kanto's strength left him as he fell to the balcony floor with a loud thump. Queen Jai'Diah rushed over to her stepfather's side. She pleaded with him to hold on and stay with her. She cried rivers of tears as she held Kanto in her arms, with his hand in hers.

"I am sorry, I thought I lost you. I thought you had betrayed me again. I am so sorry."

"Quiet now, Jai'Diah, no need to apologize. It was I who betrayed you. I have always known who you were destined to become. After we mended our relationship, I knew I had to make things right. I need you to know that I did not betray you. I was always supposed to be here with you in this fight against evil. It was foretold to me during my training with Ya'alon, The Great White Lion. Jai'Diah, I love you. You are my daughter, not my stepdaughter, but my heart and soul, my daughter. You are blood of my blood. I love you always. Now take the Golden Book from Zendor's robe and lead the people back to Yahweh." Kanto said as he struggled to breathe.

"Hold on father, do not leave me; our work is not done." Queen Jai'Diah cried.

"I am still here, my precious daughter. Take up the book and lead the people. I am right here listening."

Queen Jai'Diah arose from her father's side and walked over to where Zendor's body lay. She removed the Golden Book of Knowledge from his robe and opened the book. When she did, brightness shone all around her. She walked over to the balcony and held the book up high above her head. When she did, every greagul and wicked creature disintegrated from the illumination of the Golden Book of Knowledge.

Warriors from every tribe began to shout Yahweh as they raised their weapons in victory. Everyone helped their fellow man. Ta'nesse, Binta, and Tungo flew back down to the ground and shared in the victory. Queen Jai'Diah looked down at her people then back at her father. He encouraged her to speak the Words of the Book of Knowledge so that the great evil might be destroyed forever.

"Listen, listen!" she shouted.

"Today, Yahweh has granted us a great and mighty victory. He has reunited his people. We are all one voice now. Yahweh has entrusted me with his precious Word, the Golden Book of Knowledge. Let us not forget who has delivered us this day. Let us not forget who has restored us and returned us to our rightful place, our home. Today as I lift this book before you let us remember the ways of Yahweh and keep his Word within our hearts that we may do his will. Let us walk in his ways, the ways of truth. Father, we ask that you forgive us all, of our faults and all sins that we have committed before you. We are your chosen people, therefore let us rise

from amongst the ashes. Let us reclaim our home, which you have given us. Help us to walk in your ways so that we might prosper in all things. And it is so." Queen Jai'Diah shouted with her hands yet raised.

"And it is so" repeated the twelve tribes, after which they shouted praises to God.

Queen Jai'Diah closed the book then quickly returned to Kanto's side.

"Father, can you hear me?" She whispered as she knelt next to him.

"Yes, my daughter, you spoke well. Always allow Yahweh to guide you, Jai'Diah.

"Yes, father," she replied as tears rolled down her cheeks.

"Queen Jai'Diah heard a sound. When she turned around, she saw her husband, mother, sisters, Suncomba, Kamau, and many others standing around her. Seeing Imani, Kanto called her to him in a low whisper. Imani came forth. Queen Jai'Diah moved out of the way to give her mother space with Kanto. Imani knelt beside him.

"How is it that you are here?" Kanto asked.

"I was told that you needed me." Imani replied as tears filled her eyes.

" Tell me,, is there any hope for us?" Kanto asked.

"There is but a thought," Imani replied.

"A thought I can receive. I love you, Imani. I love our three beautiful daughters." Kanto said as he smiled and closed his eyes.

Tears streamed down Queen Jai'Diah's face as she knelt once more beside Kanto. She then lifted her head and let out a loud heart-wrenching cry to the heavens. Imani knelt beside her daughter to comfort her. Heartbroken Queen Jai'Diah threw herself across Kanto's chest, hugging him tightly. King Nayari watched helplessly, for there was nothing she could do to relieve his wife's pain.

He knelt beside her and placed his hands upon her back as she cradled Kanto's lifeless body in her arms. As she cried, Queen Jai'Diah's tears mixed with Kanto's blood. As she held on to her father, she whispered in his ear how much she loved him. Suddenly, a soft golden hue shone all around Kanto. The brightness covered his body. It looked as if the essence of the sun flowed through him; however, it was the essence of life renewed.

Kanto's life had been restored unto him, and he was completely healed. He was given new life, with a new purpose, to love purely and unconditionally. Kanto hugged his daughter and told her once more that he loved her. He then looked at Imani and smiled. Imani smiled back and said.

"There is more than a thought; there is hope."

Kanto reached out his hand and took Imani's hand in his. A single tear rolled down his cheek. Imani wiped away Kanto's tear and her own. Seeing this, Amaka and Amari ran over to their mother, father, and sister. They all shared a big warm embrace, after which Ya'alon The Great White Lion walked over to Kanto and said,

"You have proven to be an honorable Guardian."

Ya'alon then laid down at Kanto's feet.

Queen Jai'Diah walked over to King Nayari.

"Oh, how I have missed you." She said as tears flowed from her eyes.

"I have missed you too, my love." King Nayari replied as he took Queen Jai'Diah into his arms and kissed her fervidly.

Everyone clapped and shouted praises for their new King and Queen. After which, Penda and Azekel, whose Guardian name was Tungo, were reunited. Suncomba was introduced to his brother, Kamau, he never knew he had, and Azekel, another son he did not know existed. Over time, they became a close, loving family. Queen Jai'Diah enjoyed having Suncomba and Kamau as brothers and Amaka and Amari as sisters. Her relationship with Kanto deepened as her relationship with Azekel blossomed. As her family grew, so did her love for them all. Love overwhelmed her like a flood.

After the battle, everyone stayed and helped rebuild the Kingdom of Monmuket. It took a long time; however, by working together, they were able to rebuild the kingdom more majestic than before. When everything was complete, those who desired to, returned to their villages. Nevertheless, those who wished to make their home within the city walls, did so. The city grew and prospered.

Most of the Elders and Shadows returned to their sacred places. Only a few remained in the kingdom. Once the rebuild was complete Binta, and Ta'nesse decided to stick around for a little while. Jabari spent time with his family, but he eventually returned to the Dark Forest to guard Africa's most priceless treasures. Though, he did return to Monmuket from sporadically to watch over the people and help guide his royal family with wisdom.

The Guardians helped keep order as the kingdom grew. Eventually, Kanto and Imani reunited in love. They lived with King Nayari and Queen Jai'Diah in the palace, along with all of Queen Jai'Diah's siblings, who also worked within the walls. Captivated by the beautiful sunset on Ahadi, Azekel chose to build Penda, a lovely home there, on the majestic hill. There, Penda captured breathtaking sunrises every morning, each one, always more mesmerizing than the last.

Queen Jai'Diah never forgot those who cared for her. They were forever engraved in her heart. Master Keebuh and Madam Shaya held a special place in Queen Jai'Diah heart. She asked them to move to Monmuket and they did as she wished. They loved Queen Jai'Diah as their daughter. King Nayari had a palace built just for them, because of their love and kindness towards his wife.

The Kingdom of Monmuket thrived under the love and protection of Yahweh. The people devoted themselves wholeheartedly to God, through his written Word in the Golden Book of Knowledge. With Yahweh as the Head of their life, Queen Jai'Diah and King Nayari lived happily ever after with their family reunited in unconditionally love, Agape Love.

The End

Or so you may think...

Glossary

Tungo- He Who Prevails (T.L. Browning)

Abe- Father of a Multitude (Hebrew)

Yahweh- 'I AM"- "He Who Makes That Which Has Been Made" (Hebrew)

Hadriel- Splendor of Jehovah (Hebrew)

Kaijo- The Father Leads Me (T.L. Browning)

Mazena- Spirit Filled (T.L. Browning)

Jabari- Brave (Swahili)

Kei- Reverence (African)

Muji- Yishai- God's Gift- Jesse (Hebrew)

Nema- Blessing (Hebrew)

Penda-Love (Swahili)

Keradon-Place of Sadness (T.L. Browning)

Ya'alon- He will Rise Up (Hebrew)

Binta- With God (Hebrew & African)

Harun- Warrior Lion & Leader (Arabic & Hebrew)

Elad- Eternal God-Forever God (Hebrew)

Rojadaran- God Centered, Yahweh Abides (T.L. Browning)

Greagul- Rooted in Darkness (T.L. Browning)

About the Author

Tiffany L. Brown (T.L. Browning) was born in South Mississippi. She grew up in a small, quiet town. She attended Wayne County High School, home of the Mighty "War Eagles." After receiving her Associates of Arts Degree from Jones County Junior College in Ellisville, Mississippi, Brown earned her bachelor's degree from Eastern New Mexico University and later a Master's in Human Services and Christian Counseling: Marriage and Family from Liberty University. T.L. Brown now resides in Central Texas with her husband and their three beautiful children. She continues to write amazing captivating stories for all to enjoy.

Works by T.L. Browning

Jai'Diah The Lost Princess

Blood of My Blood-Wrath of the Lion

Black Noise- A Book of Poetry

Get more information about your favorite author online at

www.browningtl.com

email: tl.browning@yahoo.com

email: browningmgmt00@gmail.com

Facebook.com /browningtl

Instagram/ t.l.browning

Twitter/browningTL3

Twitter/books_roger

Books available at:

Amazon.com

BarnesandNoble.com & in store

Browningtl.com

www.ingramcontent.com/pod-product-compliance
Lightning Source LLC
Chambersburg PA
CBHW021012180626
46814CB00003B/1255